"Hey! Anyone home?"

It had been a decade since she was here, and yet the furniture was the same, the pictures the same, the same layer of dust everywhere. At the top of the stairs, she turned. Danny was probably still sleeping off some pre-birthday celebration.

"Danny? Wake up!"

She peeked in. With a grimace at the empty, unkempt room, she walked to the large window that overlooked the backyard and bay. Below there stood a glass-enclosed gazebo, a battered relic from the sixties, now at the very end of the eroding backyard, and looking as if it might topple over the cliff at any moment.

She didn't like being this high up, seeing this much wide-openness, but she couldn't shut her eyes.

Because down below, Danny lay on the floor of the gazebo, his unnatural pose and glazed stare telling her a horrible truth.

Her ex-boyfriend was very dead.

Books by Barbara Phinney

Love Inspired Suspense

Desperate Rescue
Keeping Her Safe
Deadly Homecoming

BARBARA PHINNEY

has lived in four countries in her life and never gets tired of traveling. But nowadays, you'll find her in her rural New Brunswick home writing or planning some volunteer event for her church or her children's school. The small town in which she lives provides much fodder for her stories, and she's often threatening her friends and family that they'll find a place in one of her books. Barbara has had six books published, five with Harlequin Books, and finds the Bible to be her greatest source of inspiration. She feels it has the widest variety of people, and every one of them made mistakes, yet God loved them all. That amazes her.

She would love to hear from her readers, either through her Web site, www.barbaraphinney.com or through the editor at Steeple Hill Books, 233 Broadway Suite 1001, New York, NY 10279, U.S.A.

BARBARA PHINNEY

Deadly Homecoming

Steeple
Hill®

Published by Steeple Hill Books™

STEEPLE HILL BOOKS

Steeple
Hill®

ISBN-13: 978-0-373-44320-8
ISBN-10:   0-373-44320-X

DEADLY HOMECOMING

Copyright © 2008 by Barbara Phinney

www.SteepleHill.com

Printed in U.S.A.

Bless those who persecute you;
bless and do not curse.
—*Romans* 12:14

Dedicated to my family and my friends.
Thank you, all of you. You're the best!

ONE

Northwind Island punctured the fog bank ahead. At the back of the motorboat, Peta Donald bounced on the slick wooden seat, gritting her teeth to ride out the short bumpy trip into the Bay of Fundy.

Coming home was going to kill her.

But she couldn't turn around now. Besides, Danny had called her, quite out of the blue, and asked her to come to his thirtieth birthday party. Not many ex-girlfriends got such an invitation.

And, well, after what she'd done to Danny, she had to come.

The open ferry hit another cold wave, and she cringed in anticipation of the hard bump. Salt water sprayed her, stinging her eyes and chilling her more than the early July day should.

"Sorry," the operator tossed over his shoulder. Peta swiped her face, knowing there was really nothing he could do. The choppy sea wouldn't calm just because she was on it.

By now, she could make out the wharf and some bold herring gulls searching for a free lunch. At five miles in length, Northwind Island was too small for anything but one village and one wharf. Sustained years ago by the dulse and herring industries, and now by its retirees, the island still looked the same. The trees had thickened, but the steeple of the island's only church still pierced the misty skyline.

Hopefully, she'd have time for Sunday service. Though it was Tuesday, Danny's birthday wasn't until Friday, and she'd be leaving Sunday afternoon. She should be able to manage it, and Danny wouldn't care one way or the other.

He hadn't talked to her in a year. Then, after all that silence, he'd called with his invitation. "I'm turning thirty. You've got to come and help me celebrate."

Reluctance had washed over her. "I'm hardly welcome on Northwind."

"Don't sweat it, girl. They hate everything here."

"Then why are you still there?"

Peta had felt Danny's heavy silence all the way to her Toronto apartment. "It's my parents' house," he'd finally said. "I didn't want to leave it. Not to these people."

Leave it? Peta had wondered what he'd meant by that comment, but said nothing. Instead, she'd changed the subject.

"Did you quit working for Gary Marcano?" She'd really hoped so, even after all this time. Guilt had a long memory. She should never have introduced the two men. Marcano was dangerous and manipulative, but she hadn't realized that until after the introduction.

"Oh, yeah, sure."

No, he wasn't, she'd suspected, but she hadn't felt like pushing the issue over the phone.

"Come on, Peta, girl. It's only for a few days. And I've even started to learn about this island's history. You wouldn't believe what I've found out. I want you to come. I want to see you again."

Danny had a way of coaxing. There was something in his voice and she hated what she knew would follow.

"You owe me," he'd added.

She grimaced. If it weren't for the guilt still eating at her, she'd tell him, no, thanks. But he'd remind her of how she'd introduced him to Marcano, and of how badly that had turned out.

Not much of a man, a little voice within her whispered. Danny should stop blaming her. She'd warned him that Marcano was no good a long time ago.

So why am I still letting Danny blame me?

Lord, do you want me to go home? To minister to Danny?

She'd sighed into the phone, waiting for an answer to her questions. Only long-distance silence lingered.

"Hey, Peta, come down and visit me. Take a few days off work for once. You owe me, remember?"

"Danny, don't you think it's about time you took responsibility for yourself?"

He'd ignored her question. "This is my over-the-hill birthday. You gotta come. Besides, you're worried about me, right? Come and see how well I'm doing."

Danny was intuitive enough to know that deep down, because she was now a Christian, she wanted to set things right with the people she'd hurt long ago.

"Come to my birthday party, Peta," he'd coaxed. "You can ease that guilty conscience of yours."

That last comment had cemented it.

Another wave knocked her back to the present. A minute later, the boat reached the public wharf.

The driver sideswiped one of the tires that lined the wharf, the impact shoving her against the hull of the boat. Grateful the horrible ride was over, she thanked the old man as he helped her out. At least she now knew why he'd asked for his money in advance. Hefting her knapsack onto her shoulder, Peta climbed the road that led to the village. The strap dug through her light jacket and blouse.

The café and the hardware store had been given face-lifts,

she noticed, but not the grocery store, or all the simple clap-board houses.

At the crossroads, she turned right. Two people on the cracked sidewalk halted their conversation as she passed. Old Doc Garvey and Jane Wood, the crusty grocery store owner, both glared in shock and disbelief as she stepped out onto the empty street to circumvent them.

They recognized her, and had long memories, too, it seemed. *Lord, was I wrong to come here?*

Above the noise of the constant wind, which helped to drive the tides into the bay, Peta heard the boat's engine rev up and then grow fainter again. It was clear that the ferry operator had no plans to stay on the island.

The next house on the bay side, set apart from the rest, was Danny's. Looking a bit neglected and lifeless, the two-story could have used new siding, windows and some extra-strength weed killer. Odd that Danny should want to stay here. He hadn't cared for the quiet life when they'd been young. And if he'd changed his mind since, then why not fix the house up?

Bushes rustled to her left and she snapped her head over. A branch shook in one small spot like an accusing finger wagging at her, and a shiver raced up her spine.

Abruptly, a cat jumped from the bush, and dashed away. Peta released a sigh. Coming back here was creeping her out.

Having climbed up the broken step onto the porch, she rapped on the front door. No answer. In typical small-town fashion, she pushed it open and called out Danny's name.

Still quiet. Peta fought the cold sensation crawling within her as she dumped her knapsack on the chair beside the door, and walked down the familiar hall to the kitchen.

Empty. "Hey! Anyone home?" It had been a decade since she was last here and yet the furniture was the same, the pictures the same, the same layer of dust everywhere, like some kind of unreal time warp.

Hastily, she returned to the front hall and yelled up the stairs. "Wake up, Danny. It's past noon! Get out of bed."

Never mind why he might be sleeping the day away, Peta told herself as she grabbed her knapsack and climbed wearily up the stairs. But Danny was never an early riser and she doubted he'd awaken early to greet her. He'd just expect her to be his alarm clock.

At the top of the stairs, she turned, pausing long enough to toss her knapsack onto the spare room's bed. Danny would have taken over the master bedroom now that his parents were gone. He was probably still sleeping off some prebirthday celebration.

The master bedroom's door stood ajar.

"Danny? Wake up!"

She peeked in. With a grimace at the empty, unkempt room, she walked to the large window that overlooked the backyard and the bay. Steeling herself against the vast vertigo-inducing view, she spied the motorboat disappearing into the mist. Below, there stood the glass-enclosed gazebo, a battered relic from the sixties, now at the very end of the eroding backyard, and looking as if it might topple over the cliff at any moment.

She didn't like being this high up, seeing this much wide-openness, but she couldn't shut her eyes.

Because down below, Danny lay on the floor of the gazebo, his unnatural pose and glazed stare telling her a horrible truth.

Her ex-boyfriend was very dead.

The man in front of Peta handed her a disposable mug of steaming tea. Looking at him, she muttered out a short thank-you. He then sat down on the chipped concrete step beside her, obviously taking her manners as an invitation to join her. The police officer who had answered her 911 call had asked her to leave the house, so she'd deposited her shaking frame on the broken step that began the walkway up to the porch.

"Drink it. You're frozen."

She obeyed the man, then sipped the hot liquid before saying, "I live in Toronto. We're in the middle of a heat wave right now. I'd forgotten that Northwind never gets a decent summer. Honestly, it's July 1st already. It should be warmer than this."

The man beside her chuckled and Peta stared at him. Who was he? He'd appeared shortly after the police and yet had, at some time, walked down the street to buy a cup of hot tea from the café. And while the officer and Doc Garvey went into the house, this man had stayed with her. To keep an eye on her?

He was tall, towering over her even as they shared the step. His long, jeans-clad legs stretched out before him. The sun-streaked tips of his walnut hair danced in the wind. The little wave in his hair added a contrary merriness to his somber expression. He was clean-shaven, handsome even. But his gold and green eyes carried something older and sadder. Empathy for her?

"I'm sorry," she whispered, shaking her head. "I don't know who you are."

"Lawson Mills. I'm a deacon at the church here. The police called me just to help out. But I'm the one who should be offering apologies. I'm sorry your friend is dead."

Peta acknowledged the condolences with a short nod. And appreciated that the police officer hadn't decided to keep her in the back of his patrol car. She'd been in police cars enough times as a youth. Enough to last a lifetime.

"The officer told me you said you'd come for your friend's birthday?" Lawson asked.

"Yes." Though Peta couldn't remember what she'd said to the constable. All that lingered in her mind was the image of Danny. She shivered, trying to push that image from her head— with no luck. She took another shaky sip of the hot drink.

The officer emerged from the backyard, talking on his phone. She spied him ringing off as he walked up the gravel driveway toward her. This must be quite an anomaly for the local police force. Surely Northwind had little crime now that she'd moved away. Regardless, hers had been petty kid stuff, nothing like murder.

The police would come from Saint Stephen or Saint John, two bigger urban centers. Though Northwind Island, stuck out in the Gulf of Maine, was closer to the U.S. shore, it was Canadian. The RCMP would come, as would the media.

And the islanders wouldn't like that. Not one bit.

The wind had no effect on the officer's short, gray hair as he looked down on them grimly. Lawson frowned, then stood. Peta found herself thankful that he towered over the officer. It was almost like having an ally.

And she needed an ally, especially here.

"Eventually, we'll have to go to the station so you can give a statement, Miss Donald," the policeman said. "And you'll have to stay on the island until we're done with the investigation. But you can't stay in the house like you've been doing."

Peta stood, then stepped up on the concrete tread to meet the officer at eye level. "I only just got here, Constable—" she glanced at his name tag "—Long. But sure, I guess I can find a room at the B & B."

That local inn had a name, the Wild Rose, but everyone just referred to it as the B & B. She was hoping it had a new owner who didn't know her.

The officer eyed her suspiciously. "My partner is on her

way. But it'll be a while before I can leave this property, so why don't we start your statement now?"

So there was another police officer here. Given the islanders' quirky behavior, she was surprised they'd even have two officers. These people discouraged tourists, and, if she remembered correctly, had even opposed a new wharf fifteen years ago because it might bring "troublesome mainlanders."

Peta started her statement, disjointedly giving the details of where she'd spent last night and when she'd left the mainland, all her words tasting slightly bitter, even with the hot sweet tea on her tongue.

She shut her eyes. The image of Danny still lingered in her mind. He'd aged more than she'd expected. A hard life of partying?

Oh, Lord, take that image away. Why have You imprinted it in my mind?

She'd been living in Toronto, working at an indoor construction company. She'd seen injuries, even fatal ones.

Again, as she rattled off her address in Toronto, Peta wondered why Danny had invited her. Was it really to help him celebrate his big 3-0? Because he had so few friends here? Because he knew he might die?

With another warning not to leave the island, and a receipt for her knapsack, which she'd left in the house, Peta was ordered off the property. And the officer returned to his phone.

"No place to go?" Lawson asked as she found herself dismissed at the end of the short driveway.

Feeling foolish, she shrugged. "I guess I could go down to the B & B, but I don't even have my wallet. I'll have to pay later, if I'm allowed to." With that, she started walking toward the village center.

Lawson fell in step beside her. Having lifted the fog, the

wind now blew hard in their faces. She could hear it hum the power lines above. "You said you're here to celebrate Danny Culmore's thirtieth birthday."

They passed the café before she answered, "We're old school friends, and he asked me to come back this one time, so I did."

He shook his head, his eyes unreadable in the bright, cool day. "You must have been special to him."

Was she? He hadn't spoken much to her these past few years. Peta stole a glance at the man beside her. She wanted to ask *him* what *he* was doing on the island, but held back. Ten years in Toronto had taught her not to even look people in the eye anymore. She lived in a community of strangers, all as foreign to her as she was to them. It was better to mind her own business. That way, everyone else did the same.

They'd reached the B & B. It was still the image of what it had been years ago, with huge, unruly wild rosebushes guarding its perimeter, and wind-bent trees shading one side of the large house. The wooden sign out front still rattled in the constant breeze, and, as in years before, Kathleen McPherson still sat in the front-room window, glaring out at the world from below her VACANCY sign.

Peta shook her head. It was sad to see Auntie Kay hadn't changed her bitter outlook on life.

A car growled behind them, and Peta turned. Constable Long brought his patrol car to a halt, then got out.

"Miss Donald? Can I have a word with you?"

She shot a glance at Lawson, then walked to the front of the car. "What's wrong?"

He peeled off his sunglasses and squinted against the sun and wind. "I'd like to take you to the station to ask you a few questions."

She shook her head. "I've got nothing to hide. Ask me here."

Lifting his eyebrows, he shrugged. "How long did you say you'd been here on the island?"

"I just got here around lunch, about fifteen minutes before I called 911. Why?"

"It looks like you've been here for longer. Your belongings are scattered all over the spare room. Where did you say you stayed on the mainland?"

"An inn called the Lilac Cottage. I got there yesterday morning and left around eleven this morning. I'd decided to stay there because I was tired from driving. I have the receipt in my knapsack."

He pulled out a zippered plastic bag. In it lay a handwritten receipt. "The date on this says you left yesterday. I called the inn and the woman confirmed that you'd spent one night, but had checked out yesterday, not this morning."

Peta hadn't read the receipt. She'd simply shoved it into her bag. Frowning, she shook her head. "That's not possible. I just arrived here. Ask the guy who owns the blue boat called the *Island Fairy*. He brought me here today."

The officer flipped open his notepad and scribbled down the names. "I've been told that none of the ferry boats have come in today. And I'm told that you used to live here. You dated the deceased, didn't you?"

"Yes, in high school. What difference does that make?"

"You split up with him under angry circumstances, I'm told."

The locals *did* have long memories. "True, but we settled that dispute a few months later. We were kids."

"You left here ten years ago and swore you'd never return."

"I was young and angry. But I did come back, because Danny asked me to come to his birthday."

"Anyone else see you?"

She paused. "Doc Garvey and Jane Wood saw me. Ask

them." Though with their obvious disapproval of her appearance, would they help her out, or want to see her off the island, as soon as possible?

"Anyone else invited?"

Peta wasn't sure. She hadn't received a formal invitation, just the phone call. That had always been Danny's style. With a frustrated shrug, she felt the blood surge into her face. This was stupid and confusing, and not making an ounce of sense. "I don't have all the answers. All I know is that I arrived here today because Danny asked me to come."

"Don't you find it odd that a man would ask his old girlfriend back?" the officer asked.

"This is a small community, and I was also his friend." She frowned at the officer. "What are you saying, Constable?"

The constable walked to his patrol car, then returned carrying a paper bag. "Miss Donald, is this your medication?"

He pulled out a prescription bottle. Peta took it, and peered through the clear plastic at a few round tablets. She frowned. "This is my prescription bottle, but these aren't my pills. Mine are small yellow ones. These are white."

"These were the ones found in this bottle, Miss Donald. In Danny's house."

She handed him back the bottle. "I sometimes get migraines so I carry pills to ease the pain. But these aren't my pills."

"Do you know what kind of pills these are?"

"I'm an accounting officer, not a pharmacist. They look like small aspirins."

"These are a type of hypnotic drug commonly known as the date rape drug, or 'roofies.' Several were found in Danny's mouth. The autopsy will show if he ingested any, but he appears to have exhibited the outward symptoms that this medication, when mixed with liquor, causes. And when mixed with alcohol, this drug can kill a person. Did you know that this drug is illegal in this country?"

"I can imagine! But you can see on the bottle that the medication I take is for migraines!"

The officer said nothing, but she knew what he was thinking. She could have replaced the medication with something more dangerous and offered it to Danny if he complained of a headache.

She slumped against the patrol car, battling fear and nausea. There seemed to be proof she'd been here for a least a night, *and* there seemed to be proof that she had given Danny a drug that would have at least rendered him unconscious, maybe even killed him.

Constable Long's expression turned dark. "I'd like to take you into custody, Miss Donald, to hold you for questioning in the murder of Daniel Culmore, but I have only one cell and it's got a drunk in it right now. So I'm forced to wait until backup from the mainland arrives before we can make a decision on formally charging you."

"You want to charge me? I didn't kill Danny!"

"I've also instructed all boat owners to lock their watercraft so you *can't* leave," Long continued, as if she hadn't interrupted him. "And wherever you find lodging, I'll need the address immediately."

He actually thought she'd killed Danny? Peta glanced wildly around, catching sight of Kathleen McPherson flipping the sign in her window to read NO VACANCY.

Mercy, she'd recognized Peta, after all these years.

And after all these years, this island was trapping her again. Not as a troubled youth forced to live with a long-dead aunt who cared for nothing but the support check.

No, this time, the island wanted her for murder.

TWO

A few feet away, Lawson watched Peta pale as she stared at the officer. "Are you arresting me?" she finally managed to say with a catch in her throat.

Coolness lingered in Long's expression. "No, Miss Donald, but this evidence isn't confirming your story."

Lawson took in the scene and felt for Peta. He hadn't had much to do with the law here in Canada, unlike back home in Boston. Here, the business that brought him to this island was his own, and the fewer people who knew it, the better. Especially the police.

However, Lawson regretted not having cultivated a better relationship with Constable Long. The officer was trying to gauge Peta's reaction. Right now, her reaction was very typical. She was outraged, shocked and, yes, scared.

Lawson quickly held up his hand to get the officer's attention. "What you're saying is that Miss Donald can't leave the island, and as you can see—" he pointed to the NO VACANCY sign that had, with disturbing suddenness, appeared "—there is no room at the inn, nor in the only cell you have. So why not call the mainland police to come get her?"

The officer colored slightly.

He's bluffing, Lawson thought. "In the meantime, I have

a solution. I just rented the lighthouse cottage at the cliff. It's a bit run-down, but it's okay to stay in."

"I thought you were staying up Fishing Weir Road," Long said.

Lawson kept his expression deliberately cool. "Just a change of scenery. The lighthouse and cottage are unused right now, and come as a rented set, so to speak. The owner's too old to do anything with them, so I thought I'd move. But Peta can stay there for a few nights. I've still got the house I'm renting right now." He decided not to add that the place he had right now belonged to Danny Culmore.

He felt Peta's stare settle on him. "That old lighthouse is still standing? It was abandoned years ago."

"It's a good piece of local history. The point I'm making, though, is that you need a place to stay and I'm offering the cottage. I really don't think there's any other place available."

"But is it okay for you to stay at that other house?"

"The owner won't mind." Peta didn't need to know anything more than that. Not right now, anyway.

She bit her lip and blinked. "Thanks."

He cringed inwardly as he watched how her situation was affecting her. She wasn't welcome. She was scared. And she looked like a caged animal.

The officer nodded. Just then, a call came over his radio and he turned away to answer it quietly. Lawson caught only a few garbled words, like *media, boat, two hours.*

Peta stepped toward the officer when he finished the short call. "I can't explain the receipt, Officer, but I'd like to have my knapsack back. Surely you're done with it by now?"

"I'll make sure it's delivered to you as soon as it's released. But considering these—" he held up the bagged receipt and bottle "—I can't guarantee when that will be."

Shoulders sagging, she moved away from the patrol car as Long climbed back in. Lawson watched him do a U-turn in the middle of the deserted street and return to Danny's house. A heavy sigh escaped Peta as she dropped down on the nearest bench, a few feet from where they'd been standing. She looked up at him, her expression hollow. "You didn't have to offer the lighthouse cottage, but thank you. It was very kind."

He found himself blinking at her direct stare. "It's no big deal. But the place does need some work."

"That's okay. You saw Danny's house and I was willing to stay there. I was just surprised that the spare bed was made. Danny was never very neat."

Lawson sat down beside her. "The officer thought you'd been there at least overnight. He probably thought you were being a good guest and made the bed."

Peta shook her head. She had wide, innocent eyes, the color of the bay. Her hair was cropped, messy, thanks to the wind. Its color seemed to be both caramel and coffee.

"I'd make the bed, but not pick up my things? That doesn't make any sense."

Lawson wanted to ask why her belongings were scattered to start with, but she said, "I just got here. I knocked on Danny's front door. When he didn't answer, I went in. The place looked exactly the way it had looked years ago. I'd spent enough time there to remember. There was no one downstairs, so I went upstairs. I knew Danny liked to sleep in. He…well, he partied a lot, so I figured he was sleeping it off, but he wasn't. I looked out the master-bedroom window and that's when I saw him."

"But your stuff was all over the place."

Peta frowned, then lit up. "It was! I knew right away that he was dead and went looking for a phone. I couldn't find one upstairs, so I grabbed my cell phone out of my bag. I was panicking. I threw everything out of my knapsack before I found it. Stuff got scattered.

"I dialed 911, and for some reason, got Maine's emergency instead. I must have accidentally connected to a U.S. cell. As soon as I realized that, I shut the phone and tore downstairs. I found the landline in the kitchen."

"Where else did you go?"

She shot him an odd look. Was she thinking he was a cop? The thought made him smile wryly. That was hardly the case. "I raced through the house looking for the phone," she answered. "I must have gone everywhere." She drilled him with a hard stare. "But I just got there! Once the police find that ferry operator, he'll tell them that he just brought me over."

"What about the woman at the inn who puts you there two nights ago?"

Peta shook her head, too swiftly for his liking. "I don't know why she's saying that." She ran her hands through her hair and let out a strangled noise. "This is crazy! I just arrived, I just found Danny dead and suddenly I'm the prime suspect? Do you think I would report his death if I'd killed him? I'd have left the island with that ferry operator and I'd be on my way back to Toronto by now. And I wouldn't have left any evidence behind!"

"Who thinks straight when they're killing someone?"

As soon as the question left his mouth, he knew who would. Gary Marcano, the man who he was certain had made his family disappear. And who would think straight when hiding the bodies?

Danny Culmore, as he and his investigator had begun to suspect?

Anger surged over him, and he fought it back with a gritty

prayer. His family was gone. Gone and probably dead, because the police said they'd been in the wrong place at the wrong time, witnessing the wrong thing. That was why he was here on Northwind.

To find them. To get justice for them.

Peta was staring at him. "I didn't kill anyone. And I've never seen those pills in my bottle before."

The gruesome thought of Danny's death lingered and he shook it away. He'd never liked, or even been able to deal with, graphic imagery. Years ago, in college, his buddies called him a ready-made Christian because all he could handle in movies were the mild comedies.

"Sorry."

He snapped his attention back to the present. "Why?"

"You looked like you were going to throw up. I know how you feel. Just seeing Danny dead. It was awful." The ever-blowing wind caught the strands of her hair and plastered them to her face. When she ripped them away, he realized she'd shed a few furtive tears. "I should have done more. I know CPR, first aid. And yet, I took one look down at him and just panicked."

"The doctor said there wasn't anything anyone could have done. He even tried and failed," Lawson said.

"It bothers you, though. I shouldn't have mentioned it."

"I'll live. I don't like that kind of thing, that's all. So gruesome."

She was studying him. He felt the blood rise up his neck. She had a face that was not only beautiful, but also expressive, and yet lost. Peaceful, yet hurting. An intriguing mix.

As if she realized she was staring, as he was, she cleared her throat and stood. "I guess I should make my way up to the lighthouse cottage. I don't know what to say to your offer, Lawson. It's very generous." She began to walk away.

"As the Lord expects us to be."

She spun. "You're a Christian?"

"Yes. Does that bother you?"

She smiled, letting out a soft chuckle at the same time. "No. A long time ago, I gave my life to Christ. I wasn't expecting to find anyone like that here, that's all."

"Pastor Martin would be dismayed to hear that."

"Is he the minister here? The locals—"

She stopped her words, leaving him to wonder what she was going to say. She was a local girl, had returned somewhat reluctantly, he suspected, and had almost reached the point of lashing out at those locals she'd left behind. Yet, she was a Christian, too. Again, her expressive face hinted at a complex woman.

He stood quickly, clearing his throat. "I'll drive you up to it. My car's down by the café."

"Thank you. I should walk, but frankly, I don't feel like it right now. As soon as I get my wallet back, I'll pay you some rent."

He shrugged. "Don't worry about paying me. And don't worry about your stuff, either. Let's stop at the store so you can get whatever else you need. You probably won't get your belongings back today."

"Thanks. But for that stuff, I'll definitely pay you back."

"If you like."

He led her down the short distance to the village center. Across the empty street from the café stood the small grocery store. Peta hesitated at the curb, wetting her lips and tucking a long twist of hair behind her ear. It blew free again, but this time she ignored it.

Then, catching his curiosity, she smiled briefly and strode across the street. She'd folded her arms, as if the light jacket and jeans she was wearing weren't enough for the cool summer they were having. Before stepping off the curb, he glanced around. On the road in front of Danny's house, a police car sat idling, the officer unfamiliar at this distance. Backup from the mainland? Coming up the wharf road were two newcomers with heavy black bags. Reporters. Even in Canada, they were easily recognizable.

He quickly set off after Peta.

Inside the store, she made her way swiftly down the aisles, not dawdling as he'd seen his mother do on so many occasions. She was the type to shop endlessly, enjoying the whole experience.

A sharp pang sliced through him.

Peta grabbed a toothbrush, a small tube of toothpaste, a cheap washcloth, a towel and a tiny bottle of body wash/shampoo. After that, she made her way to the counter—all business.

Rising from her battered stool behind the counter, the female clerk glared openly at her.

Even Lawson was taken aback by the strength of the scowl. Jane Wood had never displayed that kind of venom in the year he'd been here.

"Jane, how are you?" he asked, taking out his wallet to pay for what she was ringing in.

"I *was* fine." Blunt and to the point. Jane wasn't known for her gushing personality, but such overt rudeness was unusual, even for her. Her only movement was to shove up the sleeves of her plaid shirt, and to dump Peta's purchases into a plastic grocery bag.

With her head down, Peta muttered out her thanks and grabbed her newly purchased personal items. She was gone from the store before Lawson could pocket his wallet.

Out in the wind and sunshine, with his curiosity burning, he showed her to his Jeep. It was all he could do to keep his questions to himself.

Was the police officer right in suspecting this woman of murder? Her behavior told Lawson something different, but mild manners were no guarantee of innocence and people here, it seemed, knew a different Peta Donald. One who, if he was reading the hatred in Jane correctly right now, could have easily murdered the man Lawson had been seeking to bring to justice.

Peta sighed when they reached the lighthouse cottage minutes later. Up on the open meadow, the wind had free reign, bending the few black spruce and jack pine that had broken free of the forest into twisted elements from a Group of Seven painting. The slanted layers of exposed cliff beyond the retired lighthouse and its derelict companion pulled the eye down to the precarious path Lawson's Jeep bumped along.

She cringed, looking away from the high cliffs. She hated heights. And this place was too solitary for her after years of living in Canada's biggest city. No longer a part of this world, and now, returning here, she could see that the island didn't want her anymore, either.

But Danny had asked her to come back, and yes, a part of her had also hoped to somehow set things right with the people she'd hurt. Maybe she could still do that, fear of heights notwithstanding.

"Like I said—" Lawson was saying beside her as he eased up the neglected driveway toward the cottage "—the place isn't in the best of shape." They'd skimmed the cliff's edge, where the sea had stolen land from the shoulder of the lane. Peta turned deliberately away from the view.

"But I put sheets and blankets in plastic containers. And the bed is okay," he added.

"Don't worry about that. It'll be fine." She'd lived in near squalor shortly after she left home the last time. Her parents were long gone from her life; her aunt Linda had died shortly after receiving that final check before Peta had turned eighteen.

With no direction, no money and Danny deeply involved with Gary Marcano—her former boyfriend had morphed into someone she didn't want to know—Peta knew that she had to leave Northwind.

After that rough year, she'd finally turned to God. He'd led her back to where she was supposed to be.

Throwing off the memories, she followed Lawson up the short grade to the cottage. Though run-down, it still reflected the essence of its former self, a delightful story-and-a-half cottage with weathered clapboards and tiny windows peeking from the roof. The back annex had started to sag, and several windows were broken and boarded up. A rosebush, probably planted by some long-dead lighthouse keeper's wife, had begun its assault on the seaward walls, while weeds invaded the flagstone walkway. Overhead, a gliding seagull cried sharply.

Lawson unlocked the door and after pushing it open, stood back to allow her to enter first.

Immediately, suspicion rose in her. Men didn't open doors for her. She was hardly attractive enough and certainly not old enough to warrant such special treatment. Unless, of course, handcuffs limited her. Which they had, years ago.

"It's safe to live in," Lawson said quietly. "I was up here the other day, and cleaned it up, in fact."

She pierced him with a sharp look and stepped inside. Did he think she was afraid of spiders or something? They entered the kitchen, and, as he'd said, it was quite clean. Better than Danny's place.

Lawson gave her a quick tour, suggesting the most suitable bedroom upstairs, which, regrettably, looked out at the cliff, and showed her how to use the tricky shower he had yet to repair.

"But there's no food here," he said, returning them to the kitchen. "So will you let me take you out for a bite to eat?"

"Sure." Despite her easy agreement, she knew what would follow. He'd ask her why people slapped NO VACANCY signs on windows when she walked by and why the officer had automatically assumed she was guilty after hearing about her past.

Oh, well, sometimes you had to sing for your supper.

After she set her new items on the kitchen counter, they left. Lawson locked the door, took the key off his chain and gave it to her. She untied her leather necklace and slipped the key on to dangle beside a small, crudely carved wooden cross. Then the whole thing went back down under her blouse again. "I feel like a latchkey kid."

He smiled. "Just do your homework, and the only television you're allowed to watch is PBS."

She laughed back. "When I was growing up, we could only get one station and it wasn't PBS. In fact, for a while, my aunt Linda didn't bother with a TV."

They returned to town. And as the Jeep barreled straight into the village, she realized the stupid mistake she'd made.

The island had only one café. Suddenly, all the old fears and memories swept back over her. The handcuffs, the shame and the terrible sense that no one cared.

Oh, yes, the café was the last place on the island she wanted to be.

THREE

They found a table in the back, deliberately ignoring the two curious strangers parked by the window. Spying the large duffel bag with a TV station logo between them, Peta knew the man and the woman were reporters.

The small café had been redecorated sometime in the last ten years. Gone were the plastic tablecloths and brown wallpaper in that dated eighties style. Instead, the place had adopted a whale-watching theme, with old-fashioned spyglasses and framed newspaper articles hanging on the pale blue walls.

Who was responsible for this? Not too many islanders would appreciate the touristy feel. And she had yet to see any obvious tourists. Reporters didn't count.

Was this place still owned by Trudy Bell? Sitting down, Peta glanced around hesitantly. The sun that had been streaming in the long, six-paned windows suddenly dipped behind a cloud. The door to the kitchen swung open, and a waitress trudged out.

She held her breath. Trudy's longtime employee, Ellie, now made a beeline straight for them, and her expression wasn't welcoming.

She held her menus tight to her sturdy frame as she spoke

to Lawson. "We've got a good clientele here, Mr. Mills. Trudy's already told me not to serve the likes of your guest."

Peta shut her eyes as the heat surged into her face. Of course Trudy would think that way, after the vandalism.

Lawson stood slowly. "In that case, Ellie, you won't be serving me today, either." He walked around to the back of Peta's chair and pulled it out, with her still in it. "It's a shame you only serve perfect people. I'll be sure to recommend this place to the next one I meet."

Her jaw sagging, Peta rose. Lawson's hand gripped her elbow as he practically dragged her out of the quiet café. Even the reporters up front gaped at the scene.

Outside, he let her go. "We didn't have to leave, you know," she said quietly, though not wanting him to think she was ungrateful. "Ellie would have served us. Her bark is worse than her bite."

"If she wants to act like a dog, then she shouldn't be in the hospitality industry. I've worked all my life in a restaurant, at all levels, and believe me, you don't turn customers away."

He turned around, a questioning frown creasing his forehead as he asked, "What's wrong?"

"Are you for real?"

"I'm as real as you are," he said.

"I mean, as a Christian. You just told off that woman. And basically called her a dog!"

He smiled briefly. "I think you did first. All I said was if she wanted to act like one she shouldn't be working in a café. My family runs—ran—a restaurant for years. You don't treat your patrons like that." He shook his head. "Peta, being a Christian doesn't mean you should be a doormat. Or allow injustice to stand."

"But what you said—"

His jaw tightened. "Maybe I sounded a bit harsh to you, but that's the way I feel."

She thought of her congregation in Toronto, an ethnically mixed group of caring people. How would they react to hearing that she'd become a suspect in a murder? How would her minister react to what just happened in that café? He wouldn't have taken it lightly, either. "You sound like my pastor. He recently said, if I remember correctly, 'Resistance to tyranny is obedience to God.'"

"He was quoting Susan B. Anthony, an American activist," Lawson said. "So where's your church?"

"In Toronto. Downsview, actually, the north part of the city. The church I attend has a lot of immigrants, so my pastor finds himself battling intolerance from a lot of different angles. But what I meant was, so many Christians just try to maintain a strong, silent presence for the Lord. I've both admired and scoffed at that." She blinked, amazed. "I always thought I was the one more likely to overturn the tables in the temple than just make a quiet statement."

He tipped his head. "What makes you think you're a disruptive person?"

She shrugged and kept on walking. "I used to be. Hence the shunning here."

"People change." They'd reached his Jeep, and for the first time, Peta noticed the mud and peat splashed onto the fenders. No one really needed a car on the island. Twice a week—Monday morning and Friday evening, if she remembered correctly—the car ferry came over for those who needed to head to or return from the mainland. Today was Tuesday. Would she see many cars this Friday night? Would she even be here then?

Lawson opened the passenger door for her. "Where are we going?" she asked. "Is there another restaurant?"

"No, so we may as well go back to my house."

She climbed in and looked up at him as he still held the door. "You don't have to feed me."

"What kind of Christian would I be if I walked away from you now? Besides I'm hungry and you must be, too, because you didn't buy any food at the store."

A practical man—and a compassionate one—she decided. As she watched him open his door to climb in, she found herself glad that he'd stood up to Ellie.

But who was he? What had brought him here?

Once buckled in, he drove through the village, past Danny's house and up a side street that led to the fishing weirs. In the time she'd been gone, a few homes had been built on the once-empty road. Years ago, Danny's parents had owned all the land up this way. She and Danny and others used to head here on warm summer nights to party, and plan the trouble they'd eventually get into.

She hated those memories and the guilt they heaped on her now.

The driveway Lawson pulled into led to a modest, modern home. She liked the house immediately. Built of logs, it seemed to be more an appendage of its environment than a building. The rustic cabin swept down on the south-facing side, while keeping the north face tucked into the dense mix of spruce and pine.

She looked around. The house had no yard. It wasn't as if, being new, the yard might still need to be landscaped. No, the house was deliberately nestled in the crowded woods that were still standing as they had for years. Odd that someone wouldn't want even a small lawn.

She looked over at him. "Did you build this house?"

"No, I rent it."

She frowned. "This was Danny's folks' land. Did you rent it from him?"

"Danny used it as income-generating property."

She nodded. Danny preferred the easy life, leaving her to wonder once again why he'd remained on this sparsely populated island that had so little action. She turned to Lawson. "Why rent the lighthouse cottage, too? This place looks better."

A pause. "A change. The cottage has a lot of history."

His answer didn't make much sense to her. But something in it hinted that she shouldn't push the issue. Instead, she asked, "What brought you to Northwind, anyway?"

Another distinct pause. "My parents died and I needed to de-stress."

The answer was curt and brief. And a little too pat, she thought. There was clearly more to it, but she dropped the subject. She liked her privacy and would return the same courtesy.

Lawson shut off the engine. "Let's go inside. I'll make us some sandwiches. I can even give you some food to hold you over until you get to the store."

"Thanks." It was hardly his responsibility, but she appreciated the gesture. Lawson *was* being very kind to her. Too kind, almost, but after what happened at the café, she wasn't about to bite the hand willing to feed her.

Her pastor often said that to allow someone to minister to you was as good as ministering to others. Accepting help was a part of glorifying God.

Who felt rather far away right now.

Inside the house, she glanced around. Spartan, almost, with little furniture. Next to the dining room table stood a desk, on which a laptop sat closed, and papers lay scattered in an arc around it. In a far corner was a large metal detector.

Beachcombing, to de-stress, or was it for something else? Beyond was the living room, also sparsely furnished with just a couch, a chair and a side table.

After starting a pot of coffee, Lawson set everything needed for sandwiches on the dining room table. Peta, hungrier than she realized, made herself a large sandwich. They ate in silence, the only sound the coffee as it percolated and dripped into its pot.

"You know I'm going to ask why everyone on this island hates you," he said mildly after finishing half his sandwich.

"What happened to Christian discretion?"

He smiled briefly. "Did I show any of that at the café?"

True, he didn't. She eyed him cautiously. Then, knowing he may as well learn the truth from her, she began.

"I was the bad kid growing up," she started. "My parents split early on, and I went to live with my mother, but I was young and unruly, and she couldn't handle me. By the time I was six, my mother had dumped me back on the island with her older sister."

"You were born here?"

She nodded. "As was my mother, right in the clinic beside the B & B. In fact, the lady who owns the inn is my oldest aunt, Aunt Kathleen. But blood isn't always thicker than water when you're a troublemaker and a financial burden."

"Children are never a burden."

That was nice to hear, but he didn't know the whole story. "I came back to live with Aunt Linda, who never married and I know why. She was cold and nasty and told everyone that she only kept me because my mother paid her. So I grew up knowing that I wasn't loved." She tilted her head slightly at his own cautious expression. "You don't believe me, do you?"

"I can't believe that your whole childhood was miserable."

"There were some okay moments. I hung out with Danny, and we had fun at first. But he was wild, too, and I was mad at everyone. So we ended up becoming the island's trouble-makers. If anyone criticized us, we'd do our best to get back at them. My aunt would punish me, and I'd fight back. One day, the Family Services—that's what I think it was called back then—came to talk to her, but she said she wasn't going to let me go, because I meant too much to her."

"So she did care for you."

Peta laughed and shook her head. "Not quite. I heard her telling Aunt Kathleen afterward that she'd just said that because she'd asked my mother for more money, and my mother had agreed."

Lawson took a sip from his mug, a slight frown pressing his brows together. He looked comforting sitting there, his dark blue shirt open at the neck, and the sleeves rolled up to just below the elbows. Like someone she could trust.

She cleared her throat. "In all fairness, I wasn't the easiest kid to raise. I defied everyone. I set fires to brush, I vandalized buildings, and did tons of rotten stuff. Even to Danny."

Lawson's hand froze as he was setting down his mug. "Wasn't he your friend?"

"Kids aren't always nice, Lawson. I did stupid things."

"Like what?"

She looked away. Should she even be mentioning this? Would it affect her defense, if she needed one? Would Lawson go straight to the police with what she was about to say? For the first time, she thought about getting a lawyer. Why hadn't she considered that before now?

She sighed. "I went over on the mainland for the weekend once when I was sixteen. Danny followed me and we headed into Saint John for the evening. Being a port city, we figured we'd see some action. I'd met some kids there the year before when Aunt Linda went to a funeral and I had to spend time with my mom. I dragged Danny down to their place, and introduced them to him. He was looking for a job by then, and this older guy was there and just happened to be looking for someone to work for him."

"What kind of work?"

Wetting her lips, she set down her sandwich. "Selling drugs, doing odd jobs, scaring people who didn't pay what they owed him. Stuff like that. Danny was husky enough for the work." It hurt to admit, even after all these years, that she'd been the one who had gotten Danny mixed up with drug dealers.

"Drugs?" Lawson straightened. "You should tell the police that. It could be important to the investigation."

She shrugged. "It was a long time ago, and Danny said he'd quit working for Gary. It was my fault, really. I had introduced the two."

"Gary?" Lawson's word was tight.

"Yes. Gary Marcano. I wish I'd never met him. Danny changed after he started working for him. He got cocky and ruder, and had too much money."

She looked around at the sparse surroundings. "A year and a half later, Aunt Linda died and willed everything to Aunt Kathleen. I was left with nothing, so I just left. The islanders were glad to see me go."

She stood, scraping the chair along the hardwood floor. All of a sudden, she hated that she'd told her sorry story to someone who was practically a perfect stranger, as much as she hated that the old fear of being abandoned could still grip her. "I should leave. Thanks for the food. I appreciate it."

He rose. "Let me take you home."

"No. I can walk. It's still light out and I need the exercise. I'll be fine, really."

He tilted his head, gauging, she was sure, if she was really okay. "You've been through a lot today."

Finding her old boyfriend dead, being accused of his murder and then being shunned by everyone? Oh, yeah, she'd been through a lot today. "That's why I need to walk." She grabbed the grocery bag with the foodstuffs he'd put together, and stuck out her hand. "Thank you. For everything."

Lawson's warm fingers wrapped around her small, cold hand. A comforting gesture. For the briefest moment, she wouldn't have minded a hug from this man. Anything to remind her that she was…lovable.

Something that her Lord couldn't provide for her right now.

She shook away the folly and yanked back her hand. She wasn't there for any comfort. And a stranger, however handsome and helpful, wasn't going to be her lifeline. Certainly not if he lived on this island.

The only sign of life on her way to the cottage was a couple of children coloring the sidewalk outside their home with sturdy sticks of chalk. They watched her with keen interest as she stepped onto the road so as not to disturb their masterpiece.

Beyond the clinic, the road bent right and headed past the church. Her driveway plunged into the trees at a narrow lane on the left. The land around the old lighthouse and its replacement was kept clear, but at the perimeter, thick trees cloaked the lane's entrance.

Daylight was fading behind some distant clouds, so Peta quickened her step, knowing she hadn't left any lights on in the cottage and not wanting to be near the edge of the cliffs at dark. She heard a soft, rustling noise to her right, and quickened her pace. Another stupid cat, no doubt trying to freak her out.

Sea and salt caught on her tongue, telling her she was near the cliff, and that the wind had picked up. The drive in here this afternoon had been breathtaking, literally, with the road skimming too perilously close to the cliff.

But now the way felt damp and lonely and her heart tripped up several beats. She hefted up her groceries. *Don't look down. Don't look at the edge of the cliff.*

She glanced that way just the same. Her knees gelled, then liquefied. Her breath stalled in her throat. So high up, it made her ears ring. A gust buffeted her and she pushed too hard against it—

And stumbled. Then, in a desperate attempt to regain her footing, she tumbled over the cliff.

FOUR

Peta grappled with the roots and tendrils of the wild roses that clung to the edge of the island, her fear of sliding farther overcoming the painful jabs of the thorns digging into her hands.

Her foot, pedaling against the cliff face, found a rock, and she pushed hard on it, easing the agony on her hands. She threw out her right hand and met a long section of weeds. Her other foot scraped dirt and loose rocks until she'd gained another foothold.

Heart pounding, and forcing herself not to look down again, she stabilized her hold and clung to the edge. A gull, misinterpreting her actions for an offer of food, swooped close to her. She didn't need to be reminded of how high she was above the waves and water. She looked anyway, hating the self-punishment.

A gust ripped past her, trying to peel her from the cliff. Releasing the rose branch, she swung out her left hand and punctured the soft soil above with her fingers. She found cold but compliant sod, and pulled herself up a few more inches. With her foot, she scraped out another foothold and lifted herself farther. She let go of the weeds she'd grabbed wildly with her right hand and found a small log. She tossed it to one side, and then locked on to a spindly bayberry plant. Thankfully, its roots held tight.

Finally, she was able to swing her leg over the edge.

Once on the flat of the cliff, she rolled away, onto the grocery bag of food Lawson had given her. Slumped over it, she shut her eyes and waited for the cold horror within her to run its course.

Eventually, she breathed. *Thank you, Lord. Thank you so much.*

Several long minutes later, she rose, every muscle still quivering. Daylight was fading now and the rotating beacon of the new lighthouse sliced through her vision.

She grabbed her donated groceries and limped toward the cottage, her one shoe full of dirt, her opposite knee sore from scraping the cliff, and her whole front filthy.

Inside, she locked the door and slumped against it.

Hers could easily have been the next death on Northwind.

Gary Marcano. Lawson had had to fight to contain his reaction when Peta had uttered that name.

Gary Marcano was his number-one suspect. Marcano was known to police as a drug dealer and as a member of organized crime. Born in New England, but raised in Canada, Marcano had been acquitted once of second-degree murder, then became a person of interest in several disappearances, including those of Lawson's parents, his brother and his brother's family. But with no evidence and no bodies, the police could do nothing.

And now he had proof that Danny Culmore worked for him.

But Culmore was dead. And the police officer thought Peta had killed him. Where did that leave him?

Mouth tight, Lawson gathered up the dishes and began to clean up. He'd sat in his kitchen with night approaching long enough.

Peta felt guilty about introducing Danny to Marcano. *She should,* a voice inside him spat out. *Look what happened. My family is gone, probably dead. Marcano and Danny Culmore were most likely the ones responsible. Would this have happened if they'd never met?*

Forget that question. This wasn't fair to Peta.

Did she make it back to the cottage okay? She'd said she needed the walk, but with guilt eating at her and the town not wanting her back—

Ignoring the dishes, he grabbed a jacket and headed out. He would just drive up to the cottage, and if the lights were on there, he'd leave.

His heart leaped a few minutes later, when he saw the cottage blanketed in darkness. He jumped out and banged on the door. Almost immediately, Peta threw it open.

Startled, he stepped over the threshold. Only then did he notice her dirty front. "I thought I would check to see if you got home okay. What happened?"

She stared at him for a moment, then flicked out her hand in disbelief. "I fell off the cliff! Only by the grace of God did I manage to hang on and climb back up."

Cold shock sluiced through Lawson. He should have insisted on driving her to the cottage. "Are you all right?"

"A bit scraped up, but otherwise okay. I didn't fall far."

"The cliff is getting closer to the driveway with every rain. This time next year, the driveway will have to be relocated." He studied her. "It gave you quite a scare."

Peta stood stiffly. "I, um," she began, still shaking. "I'm a bit scared of heights. Well, more than a bit. I get dizzy, my heart races, and, well, this time, I fell over. I should have walked through the woods."

"You're acrophobic?"

She nodded. "I live on the ground floor of a tall apartment building, and I can't even look up at it without getting dizzy."

He stepped closer to her, feeling her vulnerable beauty like a sheer curtain whirling around her. Her eyes, dark now with relief and fear and something else, locked on to his.

"I'm sorry," she said. "Maybe I shouldn't have agreed to stay here. Even on the ferry trip over here, I was white-knuckled all the way. I can't even look out at the sea sometimes."

He wanted to pull her into a warm embrace, like the ones the little old ladies in his church back home give when someone just needs a good hug. Should he? Would she take it in the spirit it was being offered?

And what spirit would that be? a part of him wondered.

Shocked by his inner question, he stepped back, hitting the kitchen door with his heel.

She turned away, as if unaware of his thoughts. "It's this whole day. Looking out Danny's bedroom window and seeing him down there must have triggered this. I'm usually not this bad. I—I just don't like going near the edge of the cliff." She visibly shivered. "I get all dizzy."

He frowned. If this were so, how could she stand being in the gazebo, perched on a cliff, where Danny Culmore had been murdered? She wouldn't have even stepped into it, let alone been able to commit murder in it.

Peta had begun to speak again. "Maybe this is some kind of rebounding emotion from being accused of murder." She paused. "Do you think I'm guilty?"

Did he? Could she have even walked into Danny's gazebo, with it now clinging to the edge of the cliff? Another good storm and it would fall into the bay. And yet, what about the past she shared with Danny? And her reputation?

He shrugged. "No, but look at the evidence. The innkeeper

on the mainland says you were only there the night before last. To exonerate you, the police will have to find the ferry operator, but haven't yet, and your prescription bottle had the same pills found in Culmore's mouth. And you said two people saw you, but it doesn't look like they're agreeing with you."

She looked hurt as she folded her arms. "There's got to be some rational explanation for all that. Lawson, I didn't kill Danny. I swear it!"

That was the first time anyone here, except the pastor, had called on him for anything. He'd been on the island for nearly a year and in that time had taken the position of deacon at the church. To everyone, he'd come to de-stress, and he hadn't offered anything more than that, nor had the islanders asked anything more from him.

Now Peta was looking at him with a raw cry for help. She was a desperate, vulnerable woman. And a beautiful one at that. He couldn't desert her, but it was going to be hard to help her and keep his objectivity. She'd known both Danny Culmore and Gary Marcano.

He ignored the thought. "I'm sorry you've had a scare. Do you think you need to go to the clinic? Maybe get something to help you sleep?"

She shook her head. "I'm exhausted. I don't think I'll have trouble falling asleep."

"But you're alone up here. Want me to camp out on the couch?"

She eyed him silently, her gray eyes darkening again. He knew it was a bit foolish to offer to stay the night. Until a few hours ago, she hadn't even known he'd existed. Of course she wouldn't allow him to stay.

Finally, she shook her head. "I'll be okay. I just won't look out at the water." She ran her hand through her shoulder-length hair, messing it in such a way that he wanted to smooth it out. But reaching across and touching her wouldn't exactly engender trust, and he was beginning to see that she didn't have any reason to trust anyone here.

"I just need some rest," she added. "And since I can't prove my alibi, I should start looking for a lawyer tomorrow."

That was his cue to leave. She looked too tired to care anyway. He grabbed the doorknob and pulled, forcing his feet to move him out of the way, and out of any temptation to comfort her. "I'll see you tomorrow, then."

He left her, but not the property. At the point closest to the cliff, he stopped the car, and climbed out. Night had fallen, and the fog was now seeping in, though not enough to obscure his view of the cottage. He could see Peta move from room to room, closing curtains, but leaving the lights on. He glanced down at the cliff. It was getting perilously close to the narrow driveway.

The only evidence of Peta's fall lay in the crushed grass and the clumps of yanked-up weeds, both visible in his Jeep's headlights. Off to one side sat a short, sturdy log, and beside it, the sleeve of crackers he'd given Peta. He stooped to pick them up, unable to ignore the signs of leftover panic.

There was no way she could have gone into Danny's gazebo. And no way she'd be foolish enough to leave all that evidence around.

Which meant someone was framing her for murder.

Upstairs in the bedroom, with her eyes closed, Peta shut out the view of the bay, and the line of trees beyond the cottage that stood judgmentally silent, reminding her of all the things she and Danny had done. She hated the memories of the pain she'd caused the people here.

And she felt a sharp pang of loss at Danny's death, something she hadn't expected. Danny and she hadn't parted on good terms, the argument something petty and long forgotten. Though they'd made up several months later, the hard feelings had lingered between them. Now, a sense of regret swept over her.

Once notified, Danny's cousins would probably come. She could barely remember them. They lived somewhere around Fredericton. One had joined the military and was posted at the nearby base. She didn't even remember which side of the family they were from.

With tightly closed eyes, she recalled her unique view of the tree line, courtesy of her fall. In the time she'd been gone, a few maples and oaks had grown up. It would be pretty in the fall. And this lawn, more a meadow this time of year, had defied the cool temps and blossomed. Daisies and devil's paintbrush danced in her mind's eye, as if trying to calm her leftover terror.

Northwind was the perfect place for photographers and painters. Strangely, though, this small island had never attracted artsy types. The locals had refused to cultivate an openness to that kind of tourist. Why, Peta never knew. The whole island was scenic and pleasant, even with the fog rolling in on cool mornings. Photographers would love it here, but the locals preferred their island to remain quiet and unspoiled.

On the bedside table, the phone rang. She turned and stared at it. Who would be calling her at this hour? And who even knew she was staying here? To be honest, she hadn't expected the phone to be hooked up. It had to be for Lawson, as he'd already rented this cottage.

The third ring rattled through her and she reached out to grab it.

"Hello?"

A pause. "You gotta leave the island."

"Who is this?"

Another creepy pause. Her voice rose. "Who is this?"

"Drugs are bad, Peta. Look what happened."

"What are you talking about?"

"There are bad things here."

She tried to focus on the voice, but it was plain, accentless to her ear, slow and deliberate. And though she thought the speaker was male, she wasn't entirely sure. "You mean the murder? Did you kill Danny?"

"No!"

"How do I know that? Why are you warning me?"

No answer.

"Why are you trying to frame me?"

"I'm not! I saw you fall." The person let out a squeaky noise. Was this a man? "Those cliffs are bad for you. For everyone."

"What do you mean?"

There was a pensive pause. Finally, the caller spoke again. "Drugs are bad, rifles are bad. Danny's bad."

"This is crazy. You should tell the police if you know something about Danny's death."

The tone changed. The voice deepened. "'Some things are better left in civilians' hands.'"

Her blood chilled, leaving an icy hand to clutch her stomach. The whole mood switched from concern to something more sinister. Determined to ignore the melodramatic change, she snapped, "Who are you? What's your name?"

"I can't tell you no more! Just go."

The line went dead. She immediately hit the call return buttons, but a canned recording told her that the number wasn't available.

There was something else, too, something in his—or her—words, bad grammar aside. Whoever it was, one thing was certain. She'd heard that voice before. But where?

Heart thumping, she set down the phone. Should she call the police, tell them what this person had just said? Would they even believe her? Getting this call now seemed a bit too convenient.

Immediately, she thought of Lawson. But what could he do to help her? Did she even want his help?

She did. If he'd opened his arms to her tonight, she'd have walked right into them. There seemed to be a connection growing between them, some kind of odd, indefinable bond, despite the short time they'd known each other.

But that didn't mean she should call him, no matter how much she wanted to prove her innocence.

Her head starting to pound, she knew what she really needed was to crawl into bed, shut her eyes and pray that she woke tomorrow morning ready to tackle the situation God had just dumped on her.

Peta was surprised to find Lawson at the police station the next day. She'd been up early, just after dawn, a bit too early by her personal standards, but with only light curtains draped across the small bedroom window, she was awake as soon as the sun rose.

Lawson stood when she was directed down the short corridor toward Constable Long's office. Their gazes locked and she swallowed. Why was he here?

"How did you sleep?" he asked when she reached him.

"Better than I expected. I'm no worse for wear now. Why are you here?"

He frowned and wet his lips. "I need to talk to Constable Long. You mentioned that you're afraid of heights. The gazebo is very close to the cliff, almost to the point of falling into the bay."

She gasped. "I hadn't thought of that. But do you honestly think Constable Long would believe you?"

"Is there anyone in Toronto who can verify your fear?"

She'd kept her fear tucked away. The company that hired her was always looking for excuses to downsize, and a fear of heights like the ones in the plant would be grounds enough.

The closeness of the buildings in the city actually kept her acrophobic feelings at bay. Plus, she liked her solitude. It had been her best friend for a long time. Now, though… She shook her head. "Not really."

He looked grim. "Still, he needs to know."

She shut her eyes. "Danny must have known his killer." She shivered. "I can still see him in my mind. The way he looked in the gazebo. There didn't seem to be a struggle."

"Try not to dwell on that."

She glanced around. "But I know what the islanders are thinking. Being poisoned—if that's how he died—doesn't feel like a violent crime, and women prefer to kill in less messy ways." She turned to him. "But I didn't do it."

She gauged his reaction. He didn't appear to be afraid of her. And yet, he seemed determined to keep his distance.

As if to confirm her observation, he folded his arms tightly and stepped back. "So what brought you here today?"

"I needed to find out when I can have my knapsack back. I have no clothes, no money. Surely they're done with it."

"Didn't Constable Long tell you he'd drop it by?"

She glanced around at the busy station. The glass entrance doors opened onto the back parking lot, which was packed now with patrol cars. A couple of police officers she assumed were from the mainland stood talking to people whose faces were old, but familiar. She turned back to Lawson. "I want to prove that I'm not guilty. I want them to know I'm willing to cooperate."

I want to show you *that I'm innocent.*

Peta couldn't say that. Even acknowledging that she'd thought it was ridiculous. Lawson was living on this island, taking some kind of self-imposed downtime. He'd chosen Northwind. Enough reason to steer clear of him.

Still, did he believe she was innocent? Her heart beat fast at the thought.

"Hey!"

They turned. Peta watched as Tom Kimbly, who operated the hardware store now that his father had retired, hurried down toward Lawson. "Yes?"

Tom glanced down at her. Peta felt the ice in his look hit her, and turned away. It had been Tom's old car she'd vandalized once, on a stupid dare.

She'd been so immature, so foolish and fighting so much in her life. She should just offer her apologies to Tom and, after all these years, somehow start to rebuild those bridges she had burned.

Tom turned his back on her and faced Lawson. "What brings you here?"

"I need to see Constable Long."

Kimbly took his arm. "Lawson, you're a good guy. Don't be getting strung along by her stories, all right?"

"What do you mean by that?"

"I heard you left the café on accounts of her, and I can tell you, she's not worth it. She's bad news."

Lawson's eyes narrowed. "I don't judge people by what others say, Tom. And I would have thought you'd have figured that out by now."

The man looked uncomfortable. Then, obviously feeling foolish, Tom said, "Everyone knows she was involved in Danny's murder. The police here wouldn't suspect her if they didn't have a good reason."

Peta turned and walked away, choosing to ignore the man rather than confront him. If Lawson said anything more to Tom, she didn't hear it. She spotted Constable Long walking toward her, and straightened her shoulders.

"Nope, I ain't seen him in a long time. I can't tell you no more."

Peta stopped and spun. Those words. Who had spoken them? At the end of the hall, Lawson stood frowning at her. Tom Kimbly had already left the building. Through the glass doors beyond, she could see him hurrying around the corner, probably to return to his store.

All the offices and rooms were filled, with the extra police taking statements from every adult on the island, it seemed. Some doors were open, some closed, but all the conversations penetrated the thin walls.

"He was bad, he was."

That voice, again. Now she was sure it was a man. Peta pivoted. Where did it come from?

"What's wrong?"

She looked up as Lawson approached. "That voice! The same as last night. Whoever warned me off the island is here in the building!"

FIVE

"What are you talking about?" Lawson shook his head, not following her words. "Who called you last night?"

Peta took his arm and led him to one side of the narrow corridor. She held her forefinger to her mouth, and cocked her head as if listening.

What was going on? He felt himself tense up, and knew she had done the same. Her fingers were digging into his arm.

Then, as suddenly as she had dragged him to one side, she sagged and relaxed.

"What's going on, Peta? Somebody called last night? What did they say?"

She rubbed her right temple. "Last night, after you left, I got a phone call. He told me to get off the island."

"What exactly did he say?"

She repeated the conversation, and how confusing it seemed to her. "I couldn't guess if it was a man or a woman, but the person is in this building right now. I just heard the same voice! It was very distinct."

Lawson scanned the interior of the station. Like most tiny police stations, there were only a few offices, but the extra rooms and cubicles were now packed with people. Half the population of the island was here being questioned, it seemed, and with several officers from the mainland, the whole place was a beehive of activity. He'd seen Pastor Martin in one room a minute ago, and the doctor in another, plus Jane from the grocery store. Her voice was gravelly enough to pass as a man's.

But she was hardly the type to warn Peta off the island.

With a firm grip on Peta's arm, he captured her attention. "You said the caller mentioned drugs. Danny was involved with drugs with Marcano, so that can't be a coincidence. You have to tell Constable Long."

"Tell me what?"

They both turned. Constable Long stood there, calm and curious, papers in his hands and a frown on his craggy, middle-aged face.

"I need to talk to you," Peta said, rubbing her temples again. "I need my belongings, and I just want to say that if you want to interrogate me again, I'm only too happy to oblige. I can't prove that I only just arrived on this island, but I know that I didn't kill Danny."

The man's expression didn't falter. "Let's go into my office and talk."

"Wait!" She stopped him with her hand. "Who is being interviewed here right this minute?"

He flicked up his eyebrows. "Just about everyone on the island."

"No. I mean right now. Who exactly?"

"I don't know. We got a census from the municipal office and we're trying to get everyone when they're available."

"You must know who you've interviewed and when!"

Lawson frowned at her rising voice, stealing a hasty glance at the pensive officer. Peta stared earnestly at Long, while the man merely stood silently, giving away no emotions whatsoever.

Finally, he spoke. "Miss Donald, is there something you need to tell me?"

She glanced around, as if indecisive. Lawson leaned toward her, asking quietly, "You want to check out each room?"

Long threw open his office door. "No. Let's go inside. Miss Donald, I can't allow you to see who's here and who isn't. Do you want to tell me why you need to know that?"

Inside the office, watching Long place some papers on his cluttered desk, Peta repeated her story. Lawson gave her one of the chairs, listening carefully to the same statement a second time.

Long blew out a sigh. "Why do you think the caller mentioned drugs?"

"Danny had been connected to a man named Marcano a few years back. Marcano was involved with drugs and trafficking in Saint John."

"You didn't mention that before."

"He said he wasn't involved with Marcano anymore. I…I didn't really believe him, but at the same time, I didn't really have any reason not to. It's just that Danny kind of coerced me into coming back here."

"How so? How is that related to drugs or this Marcano guy?"

"Danny used people and sometimes got into trouble for it. A couple of times in the past, he blamed me for it. Small stuff, like getting kicked out of his home, or being checked by the police. We were young and ours was a bit of a volatile relationship. But after I left, I started to feel guilty about what I'd done."

"Which was?"

"I had introduced Marcano to Danny. I'd met the guy at a friend's house once, on the mainland, and I'd pushed Danny to get a job with him. But when I realized who Marcano was, I asked Danny to quit working for him. I felt bad that I'd put them together." She rubbed her forehead, looking very tired all of a sudden. "Danny picked up on that guilt, and used it against me this time. Said I should come, that I owed him because I'd gotten him involved with drugs. Danny wasn't very responsible and I guess I was overcompensating because I felt bad for what I had done. Plus, I thought God was calling me back to save Danny. Or maybe someone else here."

She looked down at her hands. Lawson could see her neck redden to a bright pink.

"And this caller last night warned you that drugs can get you into trouble, so you should leave?" Long asked.

She leaned forward, her face flushed. "It sounds weird, I know, and even a bit melodramatic. But the guy, or woman, sounded pretty earnest and sincere, like they were really trying to do me a favor." She sat back. "But I don't know why he mentioned drugs. I'm not into any drugs. The conversation made no sense to me. It was as if the guy thought I knew more than I do."

"Maybe Danny told him," Lawson suggested.

"Maybe. He said he saw me fall. But he didn't come to my rescue."

"When did you fall?"

Peta blinked at him. "I fell off the cliff last night, while I was walking back to the cottage from Lawson's house. I got too close to the edge. But listen, if that guy saw me fall, why didn't he come to help? Maybe he wants me dead, like Danny? And why was he following me in the first place?"

"Maybe he just saw you after you'd climbed back up?" Long picked up the papers he'd set on his desk. "When was the last time you were in the gazebo, Miss Donald?"

She blinked at him, looking confused at the change of subject. "I don't remember ever being in it. It was always too close to the cliff for my liking. I saw Danny's body lying there and called the police. The dispatcher told me to leave the house, so I did, out the front door."

Lawson leaned forward. "Peta has acrophobia. She slipped off the cliff last night because being high up on anything makes her dizzy."

"Then why did she walk there in the first place?"

"I needed the exercise. I walked back to the cottage, and the driveway swings near the cliff. I just didn't realize how close." She bit her lip. "I get disoriented near heights."

Long pursed his lips, set the papers down again, this time into a file. Lawson was too far away from them to read them upside down, and Peta didn't seem interested. She sat there with one hand on her forehead, as if trying to rub away her frown.

Lawson pressed on. "Constable Long, I saw Peta last night after she'd climbed back up from the cliff and she was pretty shaken up. I don't think she could even stand near that gazebo. It's only a matter of time before it falls into the bay."

"It's already started to. The bay side of it is sinking. We can only put one person at a time in it because it's too unstable." He picked up the file folder, looked at it, then set it down again.

There was something important in it. Even without seeing the contents, he read enough in the constable's body language to guess that what they'd just said either totally contradicted what was written, or underscored it. And since Long wasn't pointing out some flaw in their statements, Lawson knew instinctively that the papers somehow confirmed Peta's innocence.

He gritted his teeth, finding himself sinking deep into thought. Medication that had been switched, a night's accommodations that somehow wasn't matching up to Peta's statement. Two incriminating pieces of evidence, but also two pretty convenient ones. And what about the mysterious caller whose concern sounded more like bad movie lines than a legitimate warning?

Or a ferry operator who had suddenly disappeared? There were several private boats that could ferry people over, but the one that'd brought Peta was nowhere around. Too convenient by far.

Even Peta, as innocent as she sometimes seemed to be, wouldn't make such elementary mistakes as lying about where she'd stayed, or leave suspicious pills around to be found.

In the last year, learning all he could about criminals, Lawson knew that they sometimes took ridiculous risks and blatantly lied. But generally they took pains to cover their tracks even in murders that were not premeditated. Peta hadn't done any of that. And everything presented to her shocked her.

Long rose. "Thank you, Miss Donald. I'll get that knapsack to you just as soon as I can."

"But what about that phone call? I know what I heard, and that man is here in the building right now!"

"We'll look into it, I assure you." The constable's tone was dismissive.

Lawson rose, taking Peta's elbow. "I'll walk you home, Peta."

On their way out, with Long standing silently at his office door, Peta glanced around. Another officer, whose voice boomed, was thanking someone for coming in. Ahead, Lawson could see the doctor leaving, along with Ellie from the café. After peering in several rooms, Peta obviously realized that whoever had been here earlier had already left.

Outside, the bright sunshine hit them. The day had started foggy, but now the brightness stung their eyes.

"Ugh!" Peta said, shielding her brow.

"Your head hurt?"

"More than that. I think I've got a migraine coming on."

They'd reached the corner of the building when Long called out from the main door. They walked back, Peta keeping her head bowed.

He held out her knapsack. "I was able to get your belongings released, Miss Donald."

She grabbed the knapsack gratefully, thanked him and headed back toward the cottage again.

Lawson eyed the knapsack with a frown. "You're the first woman I've ever seen who travels light. How long were you planning to stay?"

"Until Sunday."

"For someone who had come for nearly a week, you're pretty thrifty with the clothing. One might say you weren't planning to stay long."

She stopped, shooting a glare at him from behind her palm. "What is it you're having such a hard time saying? That I knew I wouldn't be staying long because I planned to murder Danny? You're not being much help here."

Ignoring the outburst, he guided her through the town, and now they were headed toward the narrow driveway to the cottage. She had a headache and the stress was starting to make her veneer of rationality crack.

He knew he shouldn't push her. "I'm just pointing out that the police may be able to punch holes in your story. I think you need a lawyer."

Peta rubbed her temples. "I need my medicine," she snapped. "But since someone switched it, that's not going to help right now, either."

He fell into deep thought. She needed her migraine medicine, so why get rid of it all? Unless she had another bottle hidden somewhere. But the police would have found that, right? And why bother mentioning the lack of medication if she had more?

He had no answers to his questions.

"I'm sorry for snapping at you," Peta said. "It's this headache I'm getting." She stopped. "Look, if it's all the same to you, I'd rather not walk near the cliff. There's got to be another trail through the woods. Let's find it."

He'd searched nearly the whole island in the last year, on the theory that his family was buried somewhere on it. He knew all the trails. "There's another path."

They walked past the church and soon found it.

"How do you know about this?"

He tightened his jaw. "I'd seen it from the church on many a Sunday. One day, I followed it."

It was a very basic answer, with nothing about it technically a lie. But it wasn't the whole truth, either. Abruptly, the idea of holding something back from Peta didn't sit well within him.

When the trail broke free of the dense trees, they stepped into the sunshine again. With her head bowed, she hurried to the left until they reached the rear of the cottage.

There, she turned to him as she lifted off her necklace containing the door key. "I'm sorry. I shouldn't be acting so ungrateful."

He took the key and opened the door. "Apology accepted."

Inside, she sank into a chair in the kitchen. Lawson walked to the sink, soaked a clean tea towel with cold water then dug through the refrigerator for some ice. As soon as he loaded the wet cloth with the cubes, he walked back to her and eased the icy bundle onto the nape of her neck. She started, but then relaxed. He stood silently behind her for several minutes, as she sat slightly forward. The quiet felt disturbingly normal, like he *should* be helping her. Like he *wanted* to help her, for no reason at all.

Then, suddenly, Peta slumped forward.

She needed to lie down now, but the firm grip on her upper arms had other plans. "I'm taking you to the clinic. The doctor must be able to give you a shot."

She shut her eyes tightly. The sunlight pouring into the kitchen was too bright. Yes, she'd reached that point in her pain level. As if understanding, Lawson dug through his jacket's breast pocket for something, and with a peek, she discovered he was handing her his sunglasses.

"Thanks," she whispered, easing them onto her face.

Fifteen minutes later, after Lawson had retrieved his Jeep, they were at the clinic, ringing the bell at the front door. A few minutes later, an older man appeared. Peta tried to open her eyes, hating that every small movement hurt nearly as much as the car ride over.

"She has a migraine, and no medication," Lawson explained. "She needs something. And soon."

"It's bad," she whispered, keeping her head down as the silent man swung open the clinic door. "I'm seeing white spots."

The waiting room had a new coat of paint, judging by the smell that lingered beneath the scent of antiseptic.

"Don't turn on the main lights," Lawson ordered. "Are you qualified to see Peta?"

"No. I'm the caretaker. I can't give her nothing, so I have to call the doctor." Peta listened to the curt and strangely familiar voice, trying to identify it, but her head was pounding too much. With her eyes closed, all she could manage was to be guided into a chair in the examination room.

Time inched painfully by before the doctor arrived. Immediately, she recognized the voice. Doctor Garvey. He'd birthed her, treated her for all the childhood problems and once for drinking too much. While underaged, of course.

She felt the heat rise in her face, adding to the throbbing. Doc Garvey would remember it all, too, every misstep she'd taken as a youth.

He took her vitals, and assessed her level of pain as he leaned close enough to her to block out the antiseptic scent with his faint aftershave. And as expected, he said very little to her. No reason why he would, after the glare he'd given her as she walked up onto the island for the first time in ten years.

Finally, he let out a short sigh, and said, "Your mother used to suffer from migraines. They stopped after she had you. No doubt replaced by something equally painful."

The barb wasn't unexpected. Doctor Garvey wasn't known to have the best bedside manner, but being the only doctor willing to work on this tiny island, he'd been allowed to develop a surly attitude.

"Well, I'm not ready to have kids just to end these migraines," she muttered back.

"Why not? Wouldn't be the first time a woman had children for the wrong reasons. Some things should be left up to God."

It surprised her that Doctor Garvey should mention God. But she'd been away a long time, and maybe, just maybe, he'd softened a little. He went on to ask her a few cursory questions about allergies. She answered quietly, hating how his gravelly voice cut through her pain like a serrated knife. He rattled on that though he had a wide variety of pain medications available, one in particular, an intravenous drug, would work best.

Finally, he gave her an injection of something he said would be compatible with her usual medication, telling her to stay lying down with some ice on her head until it kicked in, then he left.

A few minutes later, she heard, "How are you feeling?"

She opened one eye. Thankfully, the doctor had turned off the lights, but she recognized Lawson's silhouette in the doorway. "I've been better. The doctor gave me an injection."

"He told me. He said you'll be able to go home shortly, and you'll probably sleep for at least the next day." He stepped into the room, and shut the door partway. Only a sliver of light seeped through the opening as Lawson pulled up a chair beside the exam bed.

"It's kicking in."

"The painkiller? Good. And oh, yes, Doc Garvey wants me to check in on you this evening."

She nodded, trying to work up the strength to get off the bed. "Can you drive me home?"

He chuckled. "I don't know. I'm kind of tired. Can you walk home?"

She eyed him through slitted lids. Without that chuckle of his, she'd have thought he was serious. "You'd make a good actor."

"Just a little humor to ease the pain. Ready to sit up?"

"Yes." He helped her up, his strong hands gentle and caring. Even through the fog of pain and medication, she knew she could just let him take over, be her anchor and strength and it wouldn't bother her one bit.

Her heart flipped over at the idea, and she stiffened in his arms.

"What's wrong?"

She shook her head. "Nothing. Just the pain. This medication is the best there is, but I think it's not working as quickly as I'd like it to. Don't worry, I'll be okay."

"Just as long as you can sleep. Then maybe your migraine will disappear."

"Probably. Thank you for taking me home."

"No problem."

She bit her lip. She'd just asked this guy to take her home where she'd be unconscious for nearly a day. She'd be vulnerable, as Danny had been vulnerable, out in his gazebo.

Lord, keep me safe.

No sooner had she finished the prayer than Peta stopped, troubled by a thought. The person who called her had warned that drugs were evil.

His voice had sounded all too familiar, but now, dealing with the shot and the pain, she couldn't pull the answer out of her subconscious.

Lawson eased her off the bed, and, holding her arm, led her into the waiting room. Peta was surprised to see a young woman there, rocking a small, crying child. She looked worried as the caretaker who'd let them in handed her a wet cloth and spoke to her in an unruffled, accentless tone.

Lawson thanked him, and led them outside to his Jeep. The cool, damp air soothed her face, reviving her enough to recall the details of last night, and the ominous phone call.

Joey Melanson. Because of her pain, she hadn't recognized the man who'd let them into the clinic until right then.

But now, she recognized his dull, accentless voice easily.

He'd been the one who'd called to warn her off the island. He'd known about Danny and the drugs he used to sell.

And he also knew that she was now heavily medicated and would be alone for the night.

SIX

Lawson sensed a change in Peta. Was it the medication or something else? As they drove slowly back to the cottage, her breathing quickened, and she bit down on her bottom lip. Now, weaving toward the kitchen door, she glanced around the meadow, blinking in the late-afternoon sun. She looked tired and unfocused, symptoms of the painkiller, surely.

But she also looked scared.

"Talk to me, Peta. Do you need to go back to the clinic?"

"No!" Her words slurred, she reached out her hand to grip the doorjamb. "It was Joey who called me!"

"Who?"

"The guy at the clinic."

"Are you sure?"

"Yes…and if you must know, I'm a little nervous about being up here, and out cold. Danny was drugged and murdered. I know I shouldn't be scared, or even superstitious that the same thing could happen to me, but I can't help it."

He grimaced. This was the woman who'd introduced Danny Culmore to the man he suspected of killing his family. As far as he was concerned, Danny was involved, too. Lawson just didn't know how—or how much. But could that put Peta in danger? Did she know something that could hurt whoever had killed Danny?

He forced himself to stay cool. "You're not being superstitious. In light of what's happened, I'd say you're being justifiably cautious." As he said that, he let his mind wander back to what evidence he had. A man resembling Danny Culmore had been seen talking to Gary Marcano the day before his family disappeared. Then that man was seen driving a van licensed to Gary Marcano out of Boston. A mob hit had occurred in the same area where his family was supposed to be that night.

The van was then found abandoned near a private wharf in southeastern Maine. The blood discovered within it matched his father's, but no usable fingerprints were found and, with a solid alibi, Gary Marcano hadn't been charged with anything.

Lawson fought back the wave of loss and the still unbelievable idea that his parents were probably dead, along with his brother, sister-in-law and nephew. They'd been gone a year and he continued to struggle with it. There were days that everything felt like a terrible nightmare.

Now Peta was scared that she could be a target, as well.

He didn't like the anger bubbling within him, just as he didn't like the haunting way she looked at him.

But who was he mad at? Peta? Danny Culmore and Gary Marcano? God, for taking his family?

He opened the kitchen door. "Let's go inside. You need to lie down." He steered her into the house, even as she continued to talk.

"Joey didn't kill Danny."

Joey? Oh, right, the caretaker, the one who was supposed to have called her. "Did he say that? You believe him?"

She stared at him, her gaze wavering, her pupils constricting slowly. "Sort of. I don't want to go upstairs. If the murderer comes for me, I want to be able to escape. Don't you see? I refused to take the blame for Danny's murder, and I'm forcing the police to dig deeper for the truth, so that makes me even more dangerous." She caught him with a gasp. "Wait, I need to tell Constable Long."

The medication was starting to work. Her pupils were now pinpoints of black in her dark gray eyes and yet her fingers dug into him with surprising strength. Yes, Long needed to know, but not from Peta—not right now, anyway. He'd tell the officer later.

"Lie down on the couch," he told her softly. "And don't worry about Long. You can talk to him when you wake up." He led her to the couch, pulling the afghan he'd bought at a local craft sale over her when she reluctantly lay down. Immediately, her eyelids closed and her body went limp and defenseless.

Tonight, she'd be too out of it to fight back. Lawson straightened. Did that mean he actually believed that whoever killed Culmore would come after her?

Yes, and if that person did come, Lawson would be waiting for him. Waiting and ready to extract some answers.

"I've waited long enough, Jan," Lawson said when his investigator answered her phone groggily. He'd been cooped up in his Jeep all night, but thankfully, he kept his phone charged. It gave him a chance to make a few calls, mostly to church friends who were praying for him.

"Do you know what time it is?" she snapped.

He touched his watch and the background glowed. "Four-thirty a.m."

"And do I normally work this early?" his older friend

growled sarcastically. She had a deep, strong voice, acted as tough as nails, but was soft as caramel inside. He'd seen her in action at church activities and any sad little child made her melt inside. But not in the morning.

"Your day can start very early," he answered calmly. Getting down to business, he went on, "I've reviewed some of the stuff you sent me on Culmore. Did you know he was murdered a couple of days ago?"

"Get out! Does this mean you're headed home?"

Lawson looked out at the quiet cottage. He'd locked the doors when he left and all appeared the same. "Not yet. First up, can you tell me how you made out with some of my questions? You said Culmore was doing some personal studies of recent Canadian history. So why did he end up in Boston?"

"I believe I sent you that stuff already. Didn't you get it?"

"I don't have my laptop handy so I haven't checked my e-mail."

Jan muttered something under her breath. "Well, go get it."

He glanced again at the cottage. The same lights glowed, and he'd done enough patrols around her house over the course of the night that he could safely say she was still sleeping soundly.

But he wasn't about to end his shift. "I can't right now."

Jan sighed and clicked her tongue. He could hear her stand up and shuffle around. A few minutes later, she spoke again.

"Okay. As I told you last week, Culmore had done some research into North American involvement in the Second World War. As far as I could tell, he came down here to Boston early last year to check out Maritime warfare, but why, I have no idea. There's nothing in Boston that he couldn't have found out up there."

"Early last year? Around the same time—"

"Yes," Jan answered. "The same time your family disappeared."

Lawson fought to control himself as he gritted out, "What kind of Maritime warfare?"

"Defense, surveillance, homefront navy stuff."

Lawson frowned. "Like in enemy ships sneaking into our waters?"

"Maybe he knows something we don't," she answered dryly.

"Very funny. Is your source reliable?"

"Very. He partied with the local toughs, including a few friends of Marcano's." Jan shuffled some papers. "And he knows Culmore was in Boston last year. Lawson, this is important enough for us to share with Boston PD. You should check out his house. Maybe you can find out why he was so interested in history. He must have mentioned something to somebody. He wasn't—"

Lawson gripped the phone. "Wait!" A dark figure slunk past the cottage, disappearing into the long shadow of the abandoned lighthouse. With only a half-moon out, and dawn starting, the landscape stayed dull. Even the new lighthouse beyond couldn't reach into the old one's shadow.

"Lawson, you there?"

"I'll call you back." He snapped closed his phone and shut off the interior dome light so it wouldn't come on when he opened the driver door. Leaving it open, he skirted around his Jeep and dashed over to the cottage. Peering in through a crack in the kitchen curtains, he spied Peta asleep on the couch. She turned her head slightly, but her eyes remained closed.

Lawson crept to the corner, and stared across the pale meadow. The shadow crept along the rounded wall of the lighthouse, stopping to shove his hands into his pockets.

Lawson crept past the cottage toward the lighthouse. The

shadow found whatever he was searching for and disappeared around the base of the building.

His heart pounding, Lawson dashed across the meadow. At the lighthouse, he stopped, then eased around the base, pausing again when a dim light spilled out onto the side that faced the cliff.

Times like this he wished he had a gun. But he was sure that guns had caused his parents to disappear. The use of force wasn't the answer.

At least he hoped it wasn't.

Scraping his damp palms along the rounded plaster wall, he moved toward the light. Rummaging sounds, punctuated by an occasional curse and chink of glass, filtered through the cadance of the soft surf. Someone was searching for something in the lighthouse.

He peered inside.

The island drunk, probably the one Long had mentioned. He recognized the tattered ice-hockey sweater. What was his name? Benny Something. He must have just been released from Long's holding cell. Another curse slipped from the man and then a whoop of triumph as he held up a quart bottle of liquor.

Benny kept a stash here, it seemed.

Lawson cleared his throat. The old guy jumped, spun around and in the process dropped his bottle. It hit the cracked concrete floor with a sound of breaking glass and a sickening smell of cheap liquor.

"What are you doing here?" Lawson growled.

Dismayed at his loss, Benny looked ready to cry. "I got my stuff here, that's all. Them bigwigs won't let me keep any. It's just stuff for my own use. Hauled most of it up here myself. It's bought an' paid for!"

The bottle had no label, and the liquid was clear. Moonshine. Lawson grimaced. The guy had bought a case of moonshine and with no place to store it, had somehow found a key to the lighthouse and was now using it as his personal wine cellar.

"I've rented the cottage and land, including the lighthouse. Where did you get that key?"

"I wasn't hurting nobody," the old man whined. "I had this key for years, back when I kept this place safe after it was shut down."

Lawson folded his arms. "Get this liquor out of here, tonight, or else it goes over the side of the cliff."

The man looked aghast. "It's not your property!"

"You have ten minutes to clear it out before I dump it into the bay."

The old man grabbed the stack of cases and heaved them up, groaning as he straightened. He was old and worn out by years of abusing his body, and despite his aversion to liquor, Lawson felt a wave of compassion surge over him. Ignoring the cries of anguish and fear from the old man, he grabbed the cases from him. All the way across the field he stalked, with the old guy struggling to keep up. When he reached the woods, he smacked the cases down in among the bushes. They chinked and clattered in the quiet dawn. "This stuff will kill you, Benny. Why don't you head to the mainland and check into a detox center? Maybe the doc can help you."

"Old Doc Garvey don't like me. He likes his island to stay nice and unspoiled, but I got a right to be here, too. And them over at the Saint Stephen's detox don't care about old failures like me."

Lawson doubted that, but asked instead, "Why not ask the pastor for help?"

"He don't want old drunks in his church."

Lawson knew that Benny's words couldn't be further from the truth. "I'll ask him to stop by and see you. He'd like to."

Benny tilted his head suspiciously. Then, after shooting a calculating look at the cliff's edge, muttered, "I'll think about it. Just don't throw my stuff out, okay?"

Dawn had begun to turn the eastern sky a warm scarlet. The top rim of the sun beamed across the length of the bay, and a pair of gulls above them had started their hunt for breakfast. Lawson knew this was as much of a concession as he was going to get from old Benny. "All right. But tell me something. Do you have stashes all over the island?"

"No. The rest of the island ain't good for nothing. Too much bog. Bog's too acidic an' rots the screw caps. Rots everything."

His words cut into Lawson, leaving him to swallow at the imagery. "So nobody goes into the center?"

"Why should they? Nothing there. Besides, we're fishermen. There's a boat round every bend on this island."

"Do you know anyone who would go into the center of the island?"

"Like I said, ain't nothing there. Where there's no bog, there's rock and it's no good, either." Then, grabbing a few bottles, he scampered away.

Lawson watched him melt into the forest. Then, leaving the cases and sighing, he headed back to the lighthouse. He may as well clean up Benny's mess. That way, he could keep an eye on the cottage at the same time. And after that, he'd check on Peta one more time before going home to catch a few winks. He sure needed some.

Lawson's breath hitched in his throat. He wasn't mad at Peta, but she'd had a part in the pain he felt. Anger still soured his stomach because the police had given up trying to find his family, and had scant evidence to make an arrest.

Scraping the broken glass into a discarded cardboard box, Lawson thought again about what Jan had said. Danny Culmore was studying recent Maritime history? He wasn't going to buy into the idea that the man was interested in it just for fun. Anyone interested in nineteenth- and twentieth-century history wouldn't sequester himself here on this island, where there wasn't even a library. Unless he had another motive. So what had been Culmore's?

He'd hoped to somehow worm his way into the man's confidences with a similar interest.

Too late now.

He shoved the remaining wooden boxes under the narrow stairs. They were filled with stuff that looked like moldy, prewar, lighthouse-related papers, good for nothing but to be burned. And with the broken bottle having sprayed liquor all over them, it wouldn't take much for them to ignite.

The smell of liquor burning in his sinuses, Lawson set his mind to other matters, hoping to finish his task quickly. Peta had thought that Joey Melanson, that old, slightly odd caretaker, had warned her off the island, but that he hadn't killed Culmore.

However, she was suffering from a migraine and the effects of a powerful painkiller Doc Garvey had given her. Could he trust her judgment?

Still, she had been worried and Lawson didn't like it. Nor was he prepared to analyze why he didn't. He finished his task, then opened the solitary window at the next level to allow the vapors to escape.

Dawn had offered a spectacular sunrise over the waters of the entrance to the Bay of Fundy. Last year, he'd seen several whales from this side. Now, the whole waterscape seemed to be on fire, a harsh, glaring burn on his retinas, reminding him of how long he'd been awake. Without another look at the sky, he hurried to the cottage, peeked in to find Peta still asleep, the doors and windows still secure. No one was bothering with her. He may as well go home for some rest himself.

Peta pulled herself up from the grogginess. Her mouth was parched and her eyelids felt as if they were glued shut.

But her migraine was gone. While Doctor Garvey may not like her much, he didn't fool around with medications, or offer useless solutions like ice and dark rooms. For that she was grateful.

After a shower, her energy returned, and so did her hunger. It wasn't until she was warming a can of soup that she noticed the time and date on the cable TV's info station. It was after ten at night. Amazingly, she'd slept more than an entire day. Whatever shot Doc Garvey had given her had really knocked her out.

She stopped stirring the soup. This meant she wouldn't be able to sleep tonight. What was she going to do?

Immediately, an idea occurred to her. Danny had been murdered for a reason. And that reason could still be in his house, considering Danny's lazy approach to clutter.

She gasped. *And don't forget the cubbyholes he used to use. Of course.*

Sitting down to her soup, Peta stared at the bowl. The aroma of chicken noodle seeped into her senses, along with a conviction she couldn't ignore. Breaking into Danny's house wasn't right.

Wait. Danny had invited her into his home. He'd wanted her there, and surely the police were done with it by now. That meant she, as the closest thing to a relative Danny had here on Northwind, should be allowed to go in.

There were places in that house that only Danny and she

knew about. Places the police would miss, but where Danny could easily hide what he probably had been killed for.

If the answer to his murder was hidden inside, she knew she'd find it.

The fog was in no hurry to lift. Though not as low and thick and heavy as it could be, it obscured all light, forcing Peta to inch her way along the path she'd only traveled once since her return, and with a headache to boot. Making it to the road in front of the church was the tough part. After that, she moved easily to Danny's house by memory.

Minutes later, and shooting a fast glance around the quiet, foggy street, Peta slipped up the driveway, edging along the lilac bushes and around to the back of the house.

Danny's home had practically been hers for many years, all through her troubled teens when her aunt regularly threatened to kick her out, but never did. The money her mother sent was too big an enticement. So Peta ended up here on many nights, and Danny's parents didn't seem to care much whether she stayed or not.

She and Danny had spent too many nights out and about, returning to discover the doors locked, not for security but as punishment. It made no difference. Danny had shown her several ways into the house.

Gently, Peta pushed back the large spurge plant that had grown out of control at the side of the house. This time of year it stood erect and unyielding, its hardy stalks and pale green flowers refusing to relent.

Once behind it, Peta worked at easing the glass out of its dried putty. Strange how she could practically do this in her sleep. She leaned the glass pane against the foundation and climbed in, feetfirst, easing herself down until she touched the floor. Reaching back outside, she reset the glass in its frame.

As she brushed herself off, she looked around. Danny's parents had been pack rats, keeping everything, and Danny had inherited the trait. Or else he was too lazy to bother sorting and straightening things.

More likely the latter. She'd cared for Danny, felt his death keenly, but he lacked initiative in a lot of areas.

Which begged the question of how he had managed to stay here, party and keep the house up. His parents had been no wealthier than he appeared to be, and she doubted the rent Lawson paid was substantial. Northwind Island was hardly an exotic, pricey locale, commanding a hefty rent.

Peta squeezed between stacks of boxes and old furniture until she reached the stairs. Automatically, her hand found the light switch. A dim bulb hanging on an ancient wire barely lit the cellar. She sneezed. The island dampness would send her allergies through the roof, but she'd deal with them later. Danny had several hiding places around his old family home and one was in the basement. She headed straight for it.

The loose brick at the base of the oldest section of the cellar had long been sealed with a thick, tarry substance. Obviously they'd had moisture problems in the past.

That cubbyhole was a bust. Two more to go. Both were upstairs and better candidates for hiding things, anyway.

She climbed the stairs, trying to ignore the prick of her conscience as she crept through Danny's house. It felt wrong, but she pushed away those nagging doubts about what she was doing. Danny had asked her to come and she had to find out why he had been killed.

She thrust open the basement door and slipped into the dark kitchen, turning only once to flick off the basement light.

If she found anything of importance, she'd hand it over to the police. Maybe show it to Lawson first.

Lawson. Where was he? In her mind, she had a vague recollection of talking to him about Joey Melanson yesterday afternoon. But her exact words blurred in her memory.

Peta crept along the darkened hall until she reached the stairs. The house smelled stuffy and stale. Closeness clung to her like the damp mist outside, but she forced herself to ignore it as she climbed the stairs.

At the top on the upper floor landing, she paused, reorienting herself as she decided which hidden cubbyhole to start with.

The one in Danny's old room.

She turned. Her hand still on the banister, she drew in her breath.

The scent changed into something familiar. Just a brief whiff of it in the damp, close air. Something from the bathroom, maybe? An open bottle of shampoo? No, the scent was too citrusy.

She turned, walked cautiously into the bathroom and flicked on the light.

A dark mass swept into her vision and grabbed her hard. In the next second, she was shoved face-first into the sink.

And it was filled with water.

SEVEN

Immediately, she grabbed the sides of the ancient sink, clinging hard to its slippery surface. She locked her knees and elbows.

The heavy weight of her assailant pressed terrifyingly against her arched back. Her attacker grabbed harder, shoved deeper and cursed loudly.

Peta didn't dare unlock her grip to elbow him, for fear of losing the fight.

She twisted her shoulders hard to her left, to no avail. She pushed back against his front, but her strength didn't match his.

Then, suddenly, the house shook, jarring both her and her assailant. The bathroom window rattled, and a plastic bottle of something splashed into the water. Beneath them, the floor vibrated.

The arm pressing down on her head lightened in surprise, and Peta—her heart pounding, her breath seething—twisted hard to the left. She shouldered the man, and with no conscious thought, opened her jaw against his upper arm and bit down hard.

He yelped, and released his grip. In that instant, she flipped away, banging against the door. She flung it open and dashed to the stairs.

Grabbing the banister, she tripped down the flight, hitting

the landing wall totally out of control, until she ricocheted off it and down the remaining steps. She threw herself at the front door, but it was locked tight and unwilling to open.

She pushed herself back and galloped down the hall to the back door. Twisting the lock fiercely, she knew she had only seconds before her attacker reached her. He was already on the bottom step.

The door unlocked. When she stepped back to fling it open, a big hand grabbed her hair.

She cried out. In the dark of the kitchen, she swung around wildly, until she found something long and slender.

A barbecue fork. She swung it underneath her at the right, pendulum style. It connected with his knee.

He spit out a curse, and released her. She swung the fork again, stabbing him in his midriff. Then, yanking it free, she tried again to hit his head, but her swing went wide and wild.

With a toss of the improvised weapon, she spun and dashed out the door. Dizzy and disoriented, she fell into the lilac bushes. Resistant branches gouged her arms and face.

Struggling, she freed herself, and stumbled out onto the road. Tempted to stand there and yell, she stopped.

The night had darkened, the fog thickening into a black soup.

Before it confused her way, she tore off down the newer road leading to Lawson's place. And didn't look back.

Peta. As the strange rumbling died away, Lawson's thoughts turned immediately to her. He'd slept most of the day, then read those notes Jan had sent him in the evening.

Now he needed to see if Peta was awake. If she was safe after whatever that shaking was.

But this time, he'd take his laptop in case he decided to stay the night.

Stay the night? Again?

Outside, as he reached his Jeep, he amended his thoughts. Peta was attractive, vulnerable, a Christian woman who'd found her Lord the hard way, someone whose struggle he could admire. A woman he might have, under other circumstances, been interested in dating.

But she'd also been involved with the men who might have killed his parents, and he would stop at nothing to bring each and every one of them to justice.

Because justice mattered more than anything.

"Lawson!"

About to climb into his vehicle, he lifted his head. Peta stumbled out of the fog. He rushed over, grabbing her before she fell.

She struggled for breath, and he could hear the panic in each desperate gasp.

Then she began to cry.

He pulled her against his chest. When she slumped against him, he swung her into his arms and carried her into his house.

In his living room, he placed her gently on his couch. She clung to him. "No! Don't leave! He's after me! He may have followed me down here!"

Still bending over, he held her tightly. Finally, seeing that she wouldn't release him, he sat down and held her close.

And prayed. Half out loud, half to himself, he prayed for Peta, her fear, her safety and his own strength and wisdom.

Slowly, Peta's sobs eased and her breathing returned to normal.

She was listening to his prayer. He liked holding her, so much so that he should have been praying for himself, for control and wisdom, right along with praying for her.

When he ended the prayer, she lifted her head.

"I was at Danny's house, and someone was there. He attacked me in the bathroom. He tried to drown me in the sink!"

"You were in Danny's house? How'd you get in?"

She offered him a watery expression. "I went in through a basement window."

"I can't believe the police would leave one unlocked."

"They didn't. You can remove the pane of glass because the putty is chipped and old. It's how Danny and I used to sneak in after curfew." Her smile faded. "I know I shouldn't have gone in, but I had to see if I could figure out why Danny was killed."

Tenderly, he broke their embrace, his mind racing at what she'd done. "We need to call the police."

He hadn't thought she would want the police to know she'd entered the home after they'd finished their crime-scene investigation, but with her head down and her fingers entwined, she nodded.

He walked over to the phone. "What did you hope to find that the police couldn't?"

She peeked up at him, then lowered her eyes again. "I know where Danny kept…things. When we were younger, it was his liquor stash, and later, money he got from Gary. Sometimes, at first, Gary paid him well, but told him not to put the money in a bank account. I was suspicious, but Danny said it was because Gary said he'd need ready cash."

Lawson's breath stalled in his throat. He clung to the phone. A part of him wanted to call the police and a part of him wanted Peta to keep talking.

He shook off the indecision. What was he thinking? Peta sat there bruised, hurt, scared out of her wits from a brutal attack and he wanted her to tell him about Gary Marcano. He quickly dialed 911. After speaking for a few minutes, he hung up. "Constable Long will be here shortly."

He sat down at the far end of the couch, keeping a respectable distance from her. He didn't trust himself not to pull her close, and between possible embraces, ask her about Marcano.

"We'll get to the bottom of this. But you'll need to be honest with Long, okay? About how you got into the house. And why."

"That's not a problem. I've left that other life behind. Or at least until tonight."

"You still have," Lawson said. "Just be honest with him. But you know the police are going to ask why you didn't just tell them about these hiding places before. And why you had to look in them first."

"I know. It seemed easier to go and see for myself first, in case they were empty and a waste of time. It was late, and I was wide-awake." She ended with a vague shrug.

He could hear a car approaching the house and stood. A moment later, he led Long into the house. After a few minutes of chitchat, Long asked her if she needed to go to the clinic. Peta declined. So he sat down and asked her to tell him exactly what happened.

"I thought I might find out why Danny was killed. You know, something hidden? It was stupid, I know. And I know you'll say I could have been destroying some evidence, but I didn't even get to the cubbyholes."

"How did you enter the house?"

"Through the basement window in back, behind the spurge plant."

"I'm not familiar with that plant. Where is it?"

"It's the large light green one at the center back. I removed the glass pane of the window behind it, and squeezed in, then set the pane back in again. Then it looks like it's been locked all along." She tossed a hesitant look up at the officer. "It's how we used to sneak in when we were teenagers."

"May I ask you what your relationship was with Culmore when you were teens?"

She reddened. "We dated, but really just hung out and did stuff. We weren't angels by a long shot. It was as if we were just friends, more like siblings than anything else. But that was a long time ago, and he's dead now. And that was why I broke into the house."

He pinned her with his brown eyes. "For which you may be charged."

She looked skeptical. "I doubt that. I was invited to the house, and locked out of it. I haven't compromised a crime scene because you're done with it. And I haven't committed a break-and-entry with the intent to steal, which is what the law says. I went in there to find out why Danny was murdered, not to take anything."

"And why did you think you'd find anything we'd missed?"

Lawson had been sitting quietly all this time, half admiring Peta for her ability to hold her own with Long. But that wasn't why he'd called the police. He cleared his throat. "Look, someone attacked Peta. You can deal with why she entered the house later. Someone wanted to kill her, and I'll bet it's because she's fighting the accusation of murder."

Long listened to him, then turned his attention back to Peta. "Tell me what happened when you entered the house."

"I replaced the windowpane, and then went to the cubbyhole in the basement. He used to keep liquor and cigarettes there. Later, he kept money in it."

Lawson found himself holding his breath. Would Long ask where Culmore got the money? Would Peta mention the relationship between Marcano and Culmore?

"Where is this cubbyhole?"

Peta wet her lips. "That one *was* in the basement wall

beside the wood furnace. It was a loose stone in the foundation, actually. But at some time, Danny's parents must have had the walls sealed. They're smooth and black, so that was a bust. After that, I went upstairs."

"To the main floor?"

"No. I headed upstairs." She hugged herself. "At the top, I stopped." She paused.

"Why?" Long prompted.

With a frown, she swallowed. "I was planning to go into Danny's old room. But," she said slowly, "I smelled something odd."

Long jotted something down. "What do you mean, odd?"

"Thinking about it now, I'd say it kind of smelled like cheap liquor."

Lawson held his breath. Liquor? Benny?

"Liquor?" Long asked. "When the guy attacked you, did you smell it on his breath?"

She bit her lip and hugged herself. "I don't remember. I don't think so. I walked into the bathroom, turned on the light and suddenly, there was this man grabbing me from behind. He shoved my face down into the sink. It was filled with water."

Her voice rose, and Lawson leaned forward to move toward her, but Long's sharp glance checked his movement. "I grabbed the sides of the sink and locked my elbows," Peta continued. "But he kept on pushing."

"How did you get free?"

"I twisted around. He had his arm at my shoulders, and I bit him right here." She touched her left bicep.

Long raised his eyebrows. "You bit him?"

"Yes." She gasped. "Wait! Before that, there was this odd rumbling sound, like the whole house was shaking. I think it must have startled the guy. It certainly startled me."

"Yeah, everyone felt it, but we haven't found the cause." He looked hard at her. "Go on."

She rubbed her arms. "He loosened his grip on me, and that's when I bit him. He yelled and let go, and I took off. He was going to drown me!" Her face stricken, she choked out her next words. "He was pushing my face into the sink, and I was trying to twist free! The sink was filled with water, so, yes, he was trying to drown me!"

Ignoring Long, Lawson moved to the couch, and put his arm around her shoulders. She shivered. "Constable, I know you think I killed Danny, but I didn't. And I don't care why you think I went back into that house. It was only to try to figure out why Danny was murdered. I would have shown you anything that I'd found."

"You mentioned cubbyholes. Do you think Danny Culmore was hiding something of importance in them?"

Lawson looked down at Peta, hoping the anxious feeling racing through him wasn't so evident—to either Peta or Long.

"Yes," Peta continued. "Danny used three different cubbies. Hidden holes around his house. He liked using them."

"Why didn't you tell us this before? We didn't find any secret holes."

She stiffened and moved away from Lawson. "Look, first up, I wasn't thinking of them when I gave my statement. And secondly, they wouldn't be good secret cubbies if you could find them in a routine search, would they?"

"But you went to look for them first, instead of telling us about them?"

She sighed. "I was restless. I'd woken up this evening and knew I wasn't going to sleep tonight, not after that injection Doc Garvey gave me. I'd had a migraine and needed a shot because my pills were switched, remember? I would have told you, but who's to say that you wouldn't think I planted something there before I called you about Danny's death? Or took something away? I would have looked suspicious either way. I felt guilty about breaking in, yes, but I knew I wouldn't get arrested, because I didn't have the intent to break the law. I just felt bad because it's not the sort of thing a Christian should do."

Long studied her. "What happened after you broke free of the guy? Did you get a look at his face?"

"No. It was dark, with just the street light on. I raced down the stairs and tried to unlock the front door, but he was coming down after me. So I ran to the kitchen and got the back door unlocked. He caught me there by the hair."

"What did you do?"

"I grabbed a barbecue fork and stabbed him."

"How hard?"

"Not very. He yelped, though, and backed off."

"Then?"

"I ran here. Lawson was outside by his Jeep."

Lawson could feel the temperature drop in the room, as both his guests turned to him. "I was leaving to check up on Peta," he explained. "That's why I was outside."

With his hand, Long rubbed his short, gray hair. He was obviously tired, no doubt putting in more hours than usual because of the murder.

Her stare direct, Peta leaned forward. "I can show you the cubbies I didn't get to. We can see if there's anything there that can shed light on his murder."

Lawson turned to Long. "But what about the man who attacked Peta? When she showed up here, she was hysterical. You need to find him. He may seek treatment for his bite or the stab wound."

Long nodded. Lawson could see frustration in his expression and the grim reality that maybe his prime suspect wasn't guilty after all.

The constable rose. Peta stood, too. She was much shorter than the officer, and probably half his weight, but pulled herself up to as tall as she could manage and rubbed her upper arm.

Lawson looked grim. "Are you all right? He hurt you, didn't he?"

"I must have the bruises where he grabbed me, and the bruise where I bumped into the sink."

"Do you know how your assailant got into the house? You said both doors were locked," Long said.

"I don't know." She swallowed, leaving Lawson to wonder if Long might not believe her after all.

Indignation rose in Lawson. "He could have locked the door after he entered. You know that no one here locks their doors. So he could have easily taken Danny's keys anytime. Did you find any keys?"

"Only one set. I know, that doesn't mean anything," Long added, as he tucked his notebook into his jacket. His radio, clipped to his belt buckle, crackled. "I'll arrange for some photographs to be taken of your bruises. In the meantime, we'll go to the house and you can show me the holes and go over your attack again. If you're up to it?"

She nodded. Lawson didn't care if he was invited or not, he was coming along. He picked up an oversize sweater he had draped over a chair and offered it to Peta. Her lightweight jacket wasn't going to be enough protection against the cool, foggy night.

Peta led them past the wardrobe in what she said was Danny's old bedroom. Like many old homes, the bedrooms in Danny's house had no closets. Lawson stopped at the door. Despite the seriousness of the moment, he found himself wondering if she was headed into the wardrobe in some odd reenactment of a C. S. Lewis story.

No, this was real, not some crazy fantasy. Someone wanted her dead. And someone had been here in this house for a reason. Peta had said that the sink was full of water. Why? To clean up evidence somewhere?

Peta stopped at the other side of the wardrobe. "It's here, behind the mopboard that's beside the wardrobe."

"Mopboard?" Lawson asked.

She looked up at him, her eyes wide. "This trim work. We call it the mopboard. Though it shouldn't be called that here. Danny never did any housework."

Long walked past Lawson to check out the floor. With a kit he'd brought, he quickly dusted for fingerprints, found some, and lifted them. Afterward, he wiggled the board, a tiny bit at first, then progressively more and more until it slid free from the back of the wardrobe.

Long had bent down and peered into the hole, with Lawson following his gaze. The ancient plaster didn't quite reach the floor, leaving a three-inch-high and four-inch-long gash in the wall.

"Did he make this?" Lawson asked, as Long kneeled to peer in with his flashlight.

Peta shook her head. "One of his uncles showed it to him once."

Long slipped on a latex glove, before reaching in. He pulled out a small cylindrical device on a lanyard. A piece of paper fell out with it, its shape indicating that it had been the device's wrapper.

"What is it?" Peta asked. "An MP3 player?"

"No," Long answered. "It's some kind of memory stick, I think."

It swung like a pendulum from Long's finger, and Lawson noticed the LCD number flashing on its face. He shook his head. "It's neither. It's an electronic coder called a token. They're used for secure bank accounts. The user puts in his PIN and then enters the code that's listed there. Only when both are correctly punched in can the user gain access to the account."

"I've never heard of them," Peta said, peering at it. "Do you use one?"

"No. My bank doesn't have them. But I know some Caribbean banks do, plus some in Europe and Bermuda."

Long pulled a paper bag from his pocket and dropped the device into it.

"You should take that, too," Peta suggested, pointing to the paper it had been wrapped in.

Long smoothed out the small white sheet. It was a receipt.

Lawson stiffened, recognizing the logo of a popular Boston eatery on the top. His gaze zoomed in on the date below it. At the bottom was Danny Culmore's signature, in lazy, sweeping handwriting. He'd been investigating Culmore for months now. His signature had become easily recognizable.

The date was also readable. Three months ago. The spring? Danny Culmore had been in Boston three months ago? April had been a lousy month, weatherwise, and few people made it off the island. Lawson had been watching Culmore all winter and he hadn't gone anywhere. There were days when he didn't even leave his house.

That had to be it. Those days when he never left his house were the days he wasn't even *in* his house.

Lawson felt his heartbeat accelerate to a steady thumping. What else had he missed with the guy?

Peta shot him another curious look before turning her attention back to Long as he slipped the paper into the bag. He looked at her as he folded the top of it. "Where's the other cubby?"

"In the bathroom." She swallowed.

"Feel up to going in there?" Long asked.

Lawson felt her gaze settle on him, and he tore his thoughts away from his discovery to offer a pitifully small smile of encouragement.

She nodded. They walked across the hall in single file, Peta pulling back her shoulders as she led the way.

Nothing appeared out of the ordinary in the bathroom. "It looks like no one was ever here," Long said.

"Exactly." She hugged herself. "Danny wasn't into housecleaning, but look at the sink. It's wet at the drain and someone's cleaned up after himself. He didn't want any fingerprints or proof that he tried to drown me. I just wish I knew who it was."

"You smelled liquor on him," the constable said.

"It smelled like cheap liquor, but I don't know for sure. Just something pungent."

"A strong cleaner of some kind?" Long wore a grim expression. "Show me where the cubbyhole is."

Peta pointed it out, and again Long worked at a small tile under the claw-footed tub, freeing it as easily as the baseboard in the bedroom. The hole was much smaller, not even an intentional hole, but rather a wide crack between the slabs of wood. It took some doing for Long to peer in, but he found nothing inside.

Kneeling beside the tub, Peta sighed and rubbed her arms. "I guess what you found in the other cubby will help you, but we still don't know why Danny was murdered."

The three of them said nothing, until Long broke the

silence. "We need to get your bruises documented. We have a female auxiliary officer here who can take the pictures."

She nodded. "Let's get this over and done with, then."

Constable Long took them to the police station. The police-woman seated at a computer turned and rose, grabbing her camera at the same time.

It was Trudy Bell, the owner of the café.

Peta hesitated at the door, feeling herself begin to chew on her lower lip. Long peered down at her. "Is there a problem, Ms. Donald?"

Lawson spoke. "Yes. I'd forgotten that Trudy is your auxiliary officer."

"She's only on duty when I need her," Long answered.

"She had ordered her staff not to serve us the other day." He looked directly into Trudy's eyes. "Your waitress treated Peta like a criminal, and claimed that you ordered her not to serve her. And as a police officer, you should have known better."

Long frowned, glancing back and forth between Peta and Trudy. Guilt flooded back over Peta as she explained, "I didn't leave here on good terms, Constable, and I'm sure you've been told all about my escapades. Trudy remembers me as a wild and uncontrollable kid. I vandalized her café once."

"I know your history, Miss Donald."

"Then you know why I wasn't welcomed at the café." Her next words sounded rushed even to her own ears. "I don't blame Trudy. I painted graffiti on an outside wall after she told me off. And I wasn't disciplined much. As long as my aunt got a check every month for keeping me, she didn't care what I did. It took a few hard knocks to get me on the right track. And to feel any remorse." Her voice cracked and she straightened, her mind stumbling back and forth between seeing justice done, as Lawson obviously wanted, or just running away, as Joey had suggested.

As she'd done when she first left the island? Run away from her problems?

"It's true," Trudy said, looking older and grimmer than Peta had ever seen her. "I didn't want her in my café. To be honest, I'd been working all day in the back, cooking up the meat pies for the Saturday special when I got called out to help Constable Long. I was told Peta was the one who'd found the body, and was also a suspect. I didn't want to serve her. I was tired and cranky that day. Having Danny Culmore living here was bad enough, thinking of all the things he'd done, and how he'd never felt the least bit remorseful. I was pretty much expecting the same kind of attitude from Peta." Her frown then deepened. "But I can do my job. I can document your injuries."

One of the officers from the mainland, over to assist with the investigation, peered up from a desk. Several who'd been outside, looking for the source of the rumbling, also stopped what they were doing to stare.

Behind the officer who'd just entered stood Jane Wood, her gritty demeanor even less hospitable than when Peta had entered her grocery store. She was carrying a notebook and a two-way radio, obviously there to help with the search for damage.

Peta felt Lawson's presence beside her and his hand as he gently touched her shoulder. She turned her head toward him as he said, "It's up to you, Peta."

His eyes spoke of the need for justice. He believed that she hadn't killed anyone and suddenly, running just wasn't an option.

She nodded to Constable Long. "As long as you feel Trudy can do her job, I'll accept that. I'm willing to cooperate fully. I told you that before."

Her words must have strengthened Long's faith in her. With a small smile and nod, he said, "We'll be out here waiting. In the meantime, I'll get a statement from Lawson."

After that, Peta followed Trudy into a back room.

The door clicked shut behind Trudy. They stood in the quiet room, not a space designed with aesthetics in mind. Peta had been in rooms like this one before. Questioned, rebuked, even forced at that time to make reparations. She'd had to paint the outside of Trudy's café. Paint over her "artwork."

And now Trudy was adjusting the camera for the light in the windowless room. Talk about weird. Trudy asked for a list of places that hurt, and on a piece of paper that bore an outline of a female frame, she began to jot them down.

Peta showed her the injuries on her arms and neck, listening to the older woman gasp before lifting her camera.

The picture taken, Peta pulled herself up tall.

"I'm sorry," she said quietly.

Trudy's hand had settled on the door handle. She turned back to face her. "I beg your pardon?"

"For all that I did ten years ago. I'm sorry for vandalizing your café."

"I think you apologized for it back then."

Peta couldn't hold in her smile. "Do you think that I meant it back then?"

Surprisingly, Trudy smiled back. "Not really."

"But I do now. I was a stupid kid, and ran off thinking I could conquer the world and that the world owed me. I ended up broke and turning to God for help."

"Did He help?"

Peta nodded. "Yes. But there were some hard lessons still to learn." She paused. "You've redecorated your café. It looks good, especially the framed news articles. But there aren't too many people here to enjoy it."

"I can hope they'll come someday."

Peta frowned. Did Trudy really want more people on the island? If so, she was definitely in the minority around here.

With her hand still on the handle, the older woman tilted her head. "Why did you come back? You should have just stayed away."

Was there a clipped feel to her words, or was it just Peta's imagination? Peta didn't know. "Danny asked me to and I thought that God was leading me back to minister to him."

Looking skeptical, Trudy said nothing as she opened the door. Out in the hall, Lawson and the constable looked up. The women stared at each other for a minute, before Trudy leaned toward her. "Danny was a dangerous man, Peta, and you shouldn't have come back."

"I'm starting to realize that."

"He never felt any remorse for what you both did. He bullied people, threatened them and lied to them. Didn't you know he could be lying about wanting you to help him celebrate his birthday? There could have been another reason he wanted you here, you know."

As she walked out of the room, Peta could see Lawson's interest grow. If she agreed with Trudy, knowing that Danny might have been lying to her, that could have been a motive for her to murder him. People had killed for less.

But if she said she couldn't imagine him lying, she'd be lying herself. Not an appealing option either way. And knowing Trudy was a cop prompted her to keep her mouth shut.

But she couldn't. For too many years, the guilt was bottled up inside her. "Danny had been manipulative, even without coming out and threatening anyone. He'd promised me he'd changed, not doing the stuff he'd done before. I guess I was just hopeful he was telling the truth."

Trudy shook her head. "He didn't try to mend his ways. He honestly didn't care what people thought of him. After you left, he became even more manipulative."

"He just stayed here and tormented people?"

Trudy shrugged. "He used to leave, go to Boston, I'm told. Those times were a blessing for the island." Then, as if she realized she might be saying too much, she stopped.

Peta automatically shot her gaze over Trudy's shoulder to Lawson. His frown had deepened.

"But you shouldn't have come back, Peta. It was nice and quiet here until you showed up."

"Except Danny's murder happened before I showed up, so it wouldn't have stayed quiet for long."

Trudy turned, saw the two men, and became all business again. "I'll print these pictures out tonight. Her injuries are consistent with an attack from behind. You may need more photos tomorrow. Some of the bruises may not show up until then."

Constable Long nodded and thanked her. Trudy excused herself, but turned back at the last moment. She wore that same grim expression as she had during the examination. "I accept your apology, Peta. And I'm sorry for what I said when you first got here. I've had a chance to think about it, too, and you had it hard growing up. Even your aunt Kathleen never cut you a break. Sometimes we stay angry for too long."

With that, she disappeared into another room.

Before Long could speak, Peta focused her attention on him. "If there isn't anything more, I'd like to go. But first, do you know how Danny died?"

"Suffocation, though his tox reports aren't back yet."

She wet her lips. "The same pills that appeared in my prescription bottle were in his mouth. But isn't it a coincidence that I nearly died, as well?"

Frowning, Lawson said, "And if someone suffocated him, they either did it in the gazebo, or dragged the body down there, hoping the whole building would collapse into the bay. Either way, Peta couldn't have been responsible. She can't go near it. It's too high up."

Immediately, Long folded his arms. "I can't say anything more. I'm sorry."

Trudy appeared at the door to a back office. "Your printer's out of ink," she told Long. "I have a pretty good one at the café that I use for my menus. Would you like me to print them there?"

"We don't have any more ink?"

Trudy shook her head. Peta looked around. The other officers were gone, as was Jane Wood. Gone back to searching for the source of the rumbling, probably.

"Okay, then," he answered. With that, Trudy grabbed her gear and left, without so much as a nod to Peta and Lawson.

Peta hadn't really expected one, had she? She should be taking her victories, small as they were, when they came, and even getting Trudy to smile and accept an apology was indeed a victory, wasn't it?

Fatigue suddenly weighed on her and all her joints ached. All she wanted was to soak in a tub and forget that this day ever happened.

She felt Lawson touch her elbow. His expression remained as dark as when he'd heard Trudy discussing Danny's behavior. And there was that little quirk his eyebrow gave. What did it mean? Why should anything Trudy say bother him, as it had when Peta had mentioned Gary's name for the first time, in his house?

Come to think of it, Lawson still hadn't explained why he was here. De-stressing didn't take a year, did it?

Lawson thanked Long, and opened the security door. With one last look at the officer, they walked out into the dark night.

The fog had thinned, no longer a heavy roll that the island could really boast of, but an insidious sheer. Peta knew it would thicken again. Even after years of being gone, this homecoming brought back a clear understanding of every nuance of this island's weather.

Lawson stopped in the middle of the small parking lot. He said nothing, but rather, drew her into an embrace that she could cling to like a lifeline.

Amazing. He'd known she needed one before she even knew it herself.

He was warm, comforting and strong. She shut her eyes and rested her head on his shoulder, just to savor it. Could she forget he was an unknown to her, that he'd come to North-wind for some secret reason?

No. Not yet. She peeled herself free of his arms, and muttered a short thank you.

"I figured you probably needed it," he said.

"I did," Peta said. "And you knew that before I even did. There's this little old lady at my church who hugs people. Even the shyest children run to her for hugs. She's plump and very sweet. Your hug reminded me of her."

He chuckled. "Thank you. You've just compared me to an overweight old woman."

She put her hand to her mouth. "Oh, I didn't mean it like that!"

He laughed and pulled her in for another, harder embrace. But with this one, his lips found hers.

Surprise overtook her, even more so when she felt her arms

slip around his back to hold him close. Lawson shifted his balance to accommodate her.

A popping noise sliced through the intimacy, immediately followed by the sound of crashing glass.

Lawson shoved her to the asphalt.

Another shot rang out, and Peta felt the pain instantly.

EIGHT

Chips of asphalt spat up into Peta's face. She cringed as one stung her forehead, and another her cheek. She pressed herself into the dirty driveway, but immediately felt Lawson yank her up. Her legs moved automatically as he propelled her to the far side of a police car.

She dropped down, feeling the crunch of tiny shards of safety glass digging into her knees. The windshield had been targeted?

No, they'd been targeted, but, thanks to Providence and the swirling fog, the windshield had caught the brunt of the assault.

Lawson crouched over her. Ahead of them, someone yelled. She didn't catch the words, nor would she stand to ask for a repeat.

Lawson shifted, peeking over the hood of the police car. Another round hit the left side window, then the right one, shattering both. He ducked. With her eyes tightly shut, Peta clung to the right front tire. This action did little to ease her aches and bruises.

"We should go into the police station, Lawson," she hissed as she opened her eyes. "It's not safe here."

"And get shot running in?"

"Can you see who's firing at us?"

"No, and I'll bet the whole island is out looking for damage from whatever caused that rumbling. Which means it could be anyone. We're not going anywhere," he said firmly.

"But whoever is shooting at us is taking aim from the direction of the café and grocery store. Which means they can easily run down the street and then up toward the church. If they turn right, they can shoot at us from behind."

They looked to their right. The fog, thicker now, had erased all signs of even the café next door. But an islander used to this weather didn't need landmarks to guide him. "Good point," Lawson muttered.

"Let's get inside," Peta said once again.

"Forget it. Remember what you just said? Someone from the direction of the café just shot at us."

She lifted her head from the tire. "You think it could be Trudy firing at us?"

"As good a guess as any. She did know where we were and that we'd be leaving soon."

"But it could be anyone here. We're safer inside."

He looked deep in thought. "In that case, let's go to my house. I know a shortcut."

She nodded. They bolted from their crouch and crashed into the bushes behind the patrol car. On the other side lay a small, empty lot, holding a shallow pond, something that used to turn into a muddy depression by the summer's end, but now, with the wet weather, was deep and black with the tannins of the peat that lined it.

Even now, as if in response to her thought, a light rain sprinkled down through the mist.

Another shot rang out. The bullet hit a nearby tree with a sickeningly heavy split.

Peta cried out. To the right lay a narrow path, and they raced for it. On the other side of the pond, the path melted into the woods, but when they reached it, Lawson grabbed her and yanked her down.

She landed with a thud. When she felt Lawson's weight lift off her, she turned. "What are you doing?"

"Just a sec. I want a little evidence."

She gasped as he moved toward the injured tree, pulled a small knife from his pocket and dug out the bullet. "Are you nuts?" she hissed across the distance. "That's part of a murder investigation in which I'm the main suspect, and you're taking evidence?"

He quickly returned to her. "Borrowing it. I want to see what kind of weapon fired it."

"But it'll never be allowed as evidence after this. And they'll never find the shooter, either!"

His eyebrows quirked. "They have at least two others. And as far as I'm concerned right now, they also have an auxiliary officer as a possible suspect. Come on. Let's go!" They hurried down the path, not stopping until they burst out of the woods at Lawson's back door.

Peta tripped, stumbled and fell at the base of the step. Lawson, without breaking stride, scooped her up and carried her inside.

He set her down at the entrance to the kitchen. Peta remained there, not taking off her shoes or jacket or making any attempt to enter. She just stood there, her dark gaze riveted on Lawson as he strode past her to pull the blinds on the kitchen window closed.

He turned. "Come in. Want some hot tea?"

"No, but I would like some answers."

"Of course. So would I." He tossed his jacket down on a kitchen chair, finally noticing her cautious stare. "What's wrong?"

She pulled in a shaky breath, and he knew she was struggling with something. He tried to keep his voice even. "What's on your mind?"

"I'll probably regret asking these questions, because if you've ever lived in a city like Toronto, you know enough to mind your own business, but…"

"But you were never good at following rules, even unspoken ones, right?"

"Well, that, too, but what I want to say is that I'm a suspect in a murder, and I could worry about that, or I could try to deal with Danny's death, or I could ask you a few questions. I'd rather ask you some questions."

"Ask me what?"

"First up, why are you here on Northwind? Yeah, you've already given me the de-stressing answer, but you don't look like you're having any trouble dealing with anything now. How long have you been here?"

"Nearly a year. I lost my family, remember?"

She folded her arms. "I do, and don't take this the wrong way, but frankly, it's been a year. You're not here just for that, are you? What's going on, Lawson? Why was Danny so important to you?"

Lawson stiffened. He hadn't expected Peta to be so intuitive. "What makes you think he is?"

"Because you're renting a house he owned, that his parents planned to move into before they died, plus you're being just a bit too helpful to me. And, well, just some other clues."

"Such as?"

"Like one of your eyebrows does this quirky movement when you know something. That thing we found in Danny's cubbyhole. What did you call it? A token? And the receipt. Your eyes nearly popped out of your head when you saw it.

That token must be needed for some Boston bank, because it was wrapped in a Boston restaurant receipt."

"I wasn't expecting to find a piece of relatively new technology in a secret cubbyhole. I didn't know Danny Culmore had gone to Boston last spring."

She waved her arm inconsequentially. "So what if he had? Danny used to keep an old boat over past the lighthouse. It was hidden in a small bay, not that I ever went near it, thank you. If what Trudy said was true about him going to the States, then I'm sure he would have gone that way, instead of going to the mainland, and driving down, going through customs and all that. Danny wouldn't have bothered."

Lawson couldn't believe what he was hearing. He felt his eyebrow twitch again. "He had a boat?" Did that mean illegal trips to the States? To get liquor for Benny, maybe? Why? What could Benny do for him?

She grimaced. "It's just a thought. But after ten years, the boat could have fallen apart by now." She cleared her throat. "But we're talking about you. I was going to mention your accent and how at the cottage, you talked about public television. I know you're from Boston. They talk the same way you talk there."

"Boston has more than one accent. And besides, you said you didn't have a TV growing up."

"But Danny's family did, and, remember, I spent a lot of time there. You're from Boston, aren't you?"

"Which is why that receipt caught my eye."

He knew she didn't believe him. She continued, "It's funny that Trudy said Danny went to Boston, where you're from, and you've come here. Why? It wasn't because you two were friends. And why are you so interested in Gary Marcano?"

"What makes you say that?"

"When I mentioned his name right here in your house, you lit up. Do you know him?"

"I know of him."

"And he's from Boston. When I first met him, I was warned that he had ties to organized crime."

"Which is why I know of him."

She folded her arms. "Good answer. But you worked in a restaurant. How would you know so much? I don't believe those movies about gangsters working solely out of restaurants. Why are you so interested in Danny's relationship with Gary?"

"What if Marcano killed Danny and is framing you?"

"He wouldn't have known I was coming here unless Danny mentioned it. Which means that Danny would have still been involved with Marcano and had lied to me. So maybe he lied about all the other stuff, like how he'd found something about the local history and making changes in—"

She stopped abruptly, and stared at him.

"What's wrong?" he asked.

"There you go again. Your eyebrows jumped when I mentioned Danny learning about local history. They do that when someone says something important to you."

"Really? I'm interested, that's all. What kind of history was Danny interested in?"

Her words were far slower this time and laced heavily with suspicion. "When he called me, he mentioned that he was studying local history."

He tried to keep his face still, but she was watching him too carefully. He asked, "What kind of local history?"

"Beats me. He said he'd found out some cool things, but I don't know what. I *do* know that Northwind was used for years as a place to dry fish and seaweed. We learned that in school." Finally, she stepped forward into the kitchen. "Lawson, I know you want to help me, but there's something else, isn't there? I've been accused of murdering the very guy you seem to have come to Northwind for. Don't you think I deserve to know what's going on?"

Her breath hitched and he wondered for a short, almost panicked moment if she was going to cry.

But she didn't, though her suspicious expression stayed the same. "Lawson, I know you didn't murder him. But what has Danny done? Something to do with your family?"

He held his breath. *Lord, I don't know what to do here. Help me. What should I say?*

The truth. His parents had always insisted on the truth, telling him for years that he'd never get disciplined for telling the truth.

The last day they were seen alive returned to him. "I'd called Dad's cell phone, that last day, saying that I'd meet my parents, my brother and his family at the restaurant where we were all planning to eat," he began slowly. "I had to return some DVDs we'd rented. Everyone else went ahead."

"Go on," she said softly.

"And, from what the police could tell, they'd witnessed a mob hit." His heart beat wildly. Could it have been Culmore doing the dirty work for Marcano that day?

She was staring at him, wide-eyed, full of concern, and biting her lip. He'd kept his vengeance locked tightly inside, reining it in close so it could come lashing out at those responsible for his family's disappearance, and maybe even their deaths.

Lord, I don't want to blame Peta.

"Do you want to tell me everything, Lawson?"

How could he, and not reveal how he felt? How he ached

not to blame her? But didn't she deserve to know? "My family disappeared. A vehicle was found in Maine at the coast. There was some blood, identified as my father's. When the police investigation went cold, I hired a P.I. I know from church. She found out that Danny Culmore and Gary Marcano could be involved. But the evidence wasn't strong enough to arrest either of them."

Peta hugged herself. "The Lord brought me back to North-wind for a reason. All the way down here, I thought it might be to minister to Danny. You don't need ministering to, and nobody else will talk to me. So it must be to help you."

She shrugged, wandered around, until finally settling in the chair in the dining room. Silence settled between them, cool and still like summer mornings used to be.

He fingered the bullet he was still holding. "Maybe it's just to get you to face your past. You need to let go of it."

"I know. But wouldn't it be easier to let it go in Toronto? I have a whole church willing to pray with me on that."

He set the bullet on the desk beside his laptop, which remained in its case. "Would it really be easier there?"

She smiled. "Okay, maybe I need to face these people." She paused. "If we're still here, will you go to church with me on Sunday? It would be easier then."

Still here? Where were they planning to go? "I'd love to, but remember, there's a killer out there."

"I haven't forgotten." Then, standing abruptly, she brushed herself off. "But never mind me. You've lost your whole family, and the answer could be on this island. Danny was into some bad things, but he was never good at covering his tracks. If he was involved in your family's disappearance, he must have left evidence of it here and we're going to find it."

* * *

Peta couldn't believe what she'd just committed herself to. Her words spoke of determination, of setting aside privacy, risking exposure of her seedy past.

Whoa.

She took a moment to reflect. Could Danny have murdered anyone? He just didn't seem like the type. Since he left the island so infrequently, it made no sense to travel all the way to Boston to kill someone for the mob, when they had people like Marcano right there to do that kind of horrible deed.

"Tell me what you know about Danny's boat."

"Danny used to keep a boat down past the new lighthouse. There's a small cove down there. But that was more than ten years ago. I doubt it would still be around."

"Do you know where exactly this cove is?"

"Not exactly. It couldn't be more than a small indent. I prefer to stay away from the cliffs, so Danny never invited me to go with him." She brightened. "I'll bet there's a map of the island in the lighthouse. It may show us where a boat could be hidden. Let's go."

He frowned at her. "Everyone's outside, either looking for the gunman, or helping the police check for damage after that explosion, or whatever caused the rumbling. And I'm going to help them. They'll want to know about the shooting."

"Is that wise?"

He grabbed his jacket. "Yes, we have to report it. And while I'm out, I'm going to the lighthouse. You stay here."

"All night? What about you?"

He nodded. "Don't worry about me. Lock the doors and stay away from the windows. Here's my cell number. Program it into your phone." He scribbled down a number on a small pad of paper by the computer. "What's your cell number?"

She told him. Before she could say anything more, Lawson was gone.

Slowly, she walked to the door and locked it. Then, going into the living room, she headed for the couch. There, she eased herself painfully down and let Lawson's words wash over her.

He had lost his whole family. He was only trying to find them, dead or alive.

His whole family. She couldn't imagine what it would be like to lose everyone at once. Of course, she couldn't even imagine what it would be like to have a normal family.

She shut her eyes. It made her think about how good she had it. She had a good job, a nice apartment.

And she had an accusation of murder hanging over her head.

Peta woke with a start. Bright morning light surged into the living room, banging into her with determination. She sat up, wincing at her bruises.

Where was Lawson? Surely he'd have woken her when he returned.

She rose, hurried to the bathroom to freshen up, then headed straight to the desk. She grabbed the phone and dialed Lawson's cell number.

At the second ring, he answered.

"Where are you?" she asked.

"I'm just reaching the lighthouse now."

"Where have you been?"

"I spent the night at the police station. First, giving another statement, then helping some officers inspect some buildings in the village center for part of the night. They think the rumbling was just some geological bump under the island. Not an earthquake, but what they call a bump."

"And the shooting?"

"A random act, they say. They haven't found the person responsible or even a point of origin. Half were working on that, the other half checking out buildings and people."

She swallowed. "Have you slept at all yet?"

"I grabbed a few hours at the police station. You stay there. I'll be back shortly."

She hung up, feeling relief that he was safe, but something more. An edgy restlessness. A need to do something.

Beside the phone was a phone book, which also covered several villages on the mainland. It was time for her to sort out her alibi and prove once and for all that she hadn't killed Danny. Time to take definitive action, as Lawson was doing.

Time to call the inn on the mainland.

Her heart pounding, she got through to the daughter of the elderly innkeeper on the first ring. After introducing herself, she said, "I'm the one who stayed the other day, on my way to Northwind, and you called the man who operates the *Island Fairy* for me."

The woman remembered. "Yes, that's right. He agreed to take you over there right away, even though it was a holiday."

"Yes!" Relief washed through her. "It was Canada Day. July 1. But after I got your receipt it said I left June 30."

"Oh, dear, that's not right. Mum gave you that receipt, didn't she?"

"Yes, it was a handwritten one."

"Mum doesn't like to use the computer. She's over eighty and says it's easier to do it all by hand. She must have mixed up the dates."

Even as the woman talked, Peta found things falling into place. She looked down at her watch, a simple gold-toned timepiece on an expandable strap. The date by the number three was one day behind.

The woman chattered on, but this time to her mother, who must have just come within earshot. Peta's thoughts were racing. Her watch had added a day to June. Thirty days hath September, April, June and November...

"I see the problem!" the woman bubbled on. "Mum says she asked you the date, and you told her what to write on the receipt."

"Yes, I did. And I said it was the end of the month."

She could hear the elderly woman agree. "And I looked on the calendar and saw June 30. I hadn't changed the month yet. I wasn't thinking it was already July."

Peta felt a deep sigh draw through her. The woman sounded contrite. "I'm sorry. I can see on the computer that you'd reserved a room for the night of the thirtieth, and I finished your file after Mum said you'd left. You did stay until July 1. I'll make up a new receipt for you, and pop it in the mail. How's that?"

"Good, but what I need you to do is call the police here on Northwind."

The woman gasped. "The death of that man! The reporters are saying he was murdered. My word! They don't think you did it?"

"I couldn't prove I wasn't on the island until July 1."

"Oh, dear, you were here most of the day on the thirtieth. I remember. You were so tired from driving you fell asleep on the lounge chair out back."

Peta said a quick prayer of thanksgiving for the woman's good memory.

"I'll call the police and straighten it all out," she told Peta. "Don't you worry, dear. I'll tell them everything."

Peta hung up and then sagged, tears forming in her eyes. One big hurdle overcome. She finally had a verifiable alibi. She should tell Lawson.

Getting to the lighthouse was easy, especially with the narrow trail they'd taken from the police station. Peta was able to slip past there, still a beehive of activity compared to what should have been. On Main Street beyond the station, she could see people outside. Most, she didn't recognize. Police from the mainland, here to help with the compounding trouble? Several were still inspecting buildings and the road. The geological bump, or whatever had caused the rumble, must have been felt the strongest there. But still no sign of what had caused it.

She crept into the woods behind the station, then hurried past the church. The trail Lawson had mentioned was empty and she reached the lighthouse within minutes.

"Hey."

Lawson looked up, surprised to see Peta silhouetted against the bright day, but at the same time, finding a grin creep up into his face.

Then the smile vanished. He'd been peering at a battered map and turned his attention back to it. "I thought we decided that you should stay indoors?"

"I've got good news." Quickly, she told him about her phone call.

He smiled. "That *is* good news! And I think I have some myself." He spread the map out on the floor.

She came to stand near him. "It smells in here."

He looked up at her. "Does it smell familiar?"

Her eyebrows shot up. "Are you thinking I'm some kind of closet drunk?"

"No," he answered with a laugh, "I mean does it smell like your attacker in Danny's house?"

She sniffed the air. "No. This is burn-your-eyes stuff. The other smell was almost citruslike, a bit more pleasant."

"A cleaner, maybe? Whoever it was came back to clean up some evidence."

"But the house had already been gone over by the police." She sniffed. "Why *does* it smell in here?"

"It was being used to store liquor." He began to pore over the map.

She peered down at it. "What did you find?"

"A place where Danny may have hidden his boat. Last night, while I was thinking of how you wouldn't go near the cliffs, I thought that, maybe years ago, there weren't too many places to hide a boat. But now, with erosion, there could be. The map may give us a clue to what places might erode first."

"So you're looking for any indent or natural curve of land?"

"Yes. If Danny was smuggling liquor, he would have to be secretive, but still not too far from where he was hiding it."

"Makes sense. But who would Danny sell the stuff to? By the sounds of it, the rest of the islanders wouldn't have anything to do with him."

Lawson frowned, thinking of Benny. "Or hated him enough to kill him?"

"I don't know. But I know that one big alibi problem with me has been solved, and I want to help you now. I want to help you find out what happened to your family."

He swallowed. Grief and some other emotion he didn't want to scrutinize trickled through him. He turned back to the map. "There's one here, about half a mile away."

She knelt down beside him. "I noticed that the trail to this lighthouse splits about halfway, and it looks relatively new. I bet it goes to that little cove."

"Let's go."

Her shoulders sagged a bit. "I'll follow you as far as I can, okay? I mean, I want to help you find your family, but…" She smiled sheepishly.

He wanted to comfort her, but revenge had percolated inside him for a year and he clung to it as a source of energy, of motivation. To keep him focused. Up until this last week, he hadn't found any solid, usable evidence of Danny's involvement in his family's disappearance. Now Peta had revealed an array of clues and hints to sort through, while at the same time, in her own way, showing how important it was to let go of the past and start living for the future.

He told himself he'd deal with his feelings for Peta after he'd found the boat. *Okay, Lord? I'll sort it out later.*

Peta shook her head. "Don't get your hopes up. Remember that Danny may not have a boat anymore." She paused. "And I wish I could climb down the cliff to help you look."

"You can be the lookout." He thought of the bullet and sighed. "And I want to compare the round with the ones used in the hit that my family witnessed."

"You think Marcano was the hit man, and the one who killed Danny? If you take that bullet to the Boston PD they'll ask you where you got it. What will you say?"

Who knows, he thought dejectedly. And how would he get it there? With no one on the island he could trust to take it, the only other option would be to send it to Jan by courier from a neutral location.

That would leave Peta alone on Northwind.

And what about how you tampered with evidence?

Oblivious to his thoughts, Peta stepped outside. "Never mind the bullet right now. We'll look for the boat."

"Would you believe that this whole section is called Shelter Cove?" Peta asked a few minutes later as they trudged along the overgrown path. She was carrying the map and studying it as they walked.

The new lighthouse, a much smaller, more efficient one, stood at the southwest corner of the island. Today, the fog was gone, the bright sun washing the landscape in light.

Maybe they'd finally get some decent weather.

"I wonder why it was called Shelter Cove when it was no more than an indent back when this map was printed," Lawson said.

"Beats me. Maybe they thought it could be something someday. Or someone's idea of a joke." Peta shrugged. "Who knows?"

"What about the cove at the end of my road where the fishing weirs are?" he asked.

"Technically, that's a bay. Don't ask me the difference. Maybe size, but there's nothing big on this island." She gave one quick sweep across the horizon, then with a deep breath, began to walk toward a jagged spit of land. A trio of gulls circled lazily above them.

Lawson looked to his left across the water. "That's Grand Manan Island?"

"Yes, and over there—" she pointed to her right, where the land was closer and more visible "—is the States. Come on. You'd better hope that the cove hasn't eroded to nothing."

It nearly had been, Lawson discovered. Leaving Peta up top, far from the edge, and sitting down, he slid and scraped his way down the cliff. At one point, a jut of harder rock, less prone to erosion, formed a ledge.

He jumped onto it, and then onto another ledge. The sea and wind had carved a shallow cave out of the softer sandstone below. He jumped down to the sandy shore.

A tall section of rock sheltered the tiny crescent of beach

from the wind, and Lawson headed to the crack it made in the land that could, within a decade, form a small flowerpot island of its own. There sat a small, battered aluminum boat, complete with a twenty-horsepower outboard motor pulled up higher than the tide.

Lawson found his heart pounding as he walked closer to it.

He flipped open his cell phone and dialed Peta's. "I found a boat. I can't believe that Danny was the only one to use this cove," he said when she answered.

"The bay on the other side is easier to access, and has calmer water. When the tide rushes in, it goes right past here, around the cliff where I fell, past Campobello Island, and up to the Old Sow."

He'd heard of the currents in this area and the resulting whirlpool. "How dangerous are the tides?"

"Very, if you're not careful. Even my aunt wouldn't allow me to come down by the water. And local fishermen steered clear of this side of the island when the tide was turning. The Old Sow is the largest whirlpool in the Western Hemisphere, and acts like a magnet for the water that comes through here. Danny told me once there are some piglets here, too."

"Piglets?"

"Smaller whirlpools. It's really the term used for those around Old Sow. But at certain moon phases, the ones here are known to knock small boats off course, or if you're traveling fast enough, tip you over. This side of the island is so deadly that they had to put up the lighthouse."

"So nobody comes around this way?"

"What's here except unmanageable waters and high cliffs? Most people choose the bay on the other side, if they want to go to the States, or do any boating. But they usually just stay around Northwind."

"There's certainly a feel of protectiveness here." He'd noticed that attitude in the islanders. The only one who was tolerated to wrestle with it was the pastor. But the poor guy had to face that attitude every Sunday.

And he was tolerated—nothing more.

Dismissing the thought, Lawson leaned into the boat.

While the wind blew less forceful than at the top of the cliff, the air had once again turned damp and cold.

"Whoever uses the boat would probably keep his gas tank down there," Peta was saying into her phone. "It's got to be somewhere nearby."

He looked around, then climbed up on a few rocks before saying into his phone, "It's here, hidden in a crevice."

He turned his attention back to the boat. Heat-absorbing seats, flotation blocks and, for essentials, a small compartment under the backseat by the motor.

Setting his phone down on the seat, he tugged the compartment open. Its contents spilled out onto the slightly curved bottom.

Peta's voice reached him. "What are you doing?"

"Opening the only compartment to see if I can find anything that might tell us if Danny had been going to the States regularly. It might point to a killer."

"Do you think that someone came here from Maine to kill him? Like Gary Marcano?"

He picked up the phone. "Why do you think Gary Marcano would want to kill Danny? You know both of them."

"Danny said he was done with Gary, but from what Trudy said, he might have been lying. I mean, why go to Boston except to see Gary? And if he had money in a secret bank account, he must have done some work for the guy. Maybe

Gary got jealous, or Danny stole from him," Peta reflected. "In one way, it's hard to imagine. In another way, it's not."

She sounded hurt, distressed at the notion that Danny hadn't changed much in the years she'd been gone. Lawson thought of setting aside the task at hand to climb up the cliff and pull her into a warm embrace that would be as much for him as for her.

Setting aside the thought, he flicked the contents of the compartment around a bit, seeing mostly the required safety gear—flashlight, whistle, first-aid kit, all in a bailer bucket— along with papers and garbage and other small items.

A thin square of leather flopped open. In its plastic window, a faded photo of two smiling men beamed up at him.

He gasped.

"What's wrong?" Peta asked swiftly.

"It's my father's wallet."

NINE

The photo showed Lawson with his brother, taken two summers before at a mainland amusement park. Lawson's throat constricted. The whole family had gone there; his brother and sister-in-law had taken their son, too. His nephew had snapped the picture with a cheap disposable camera and it had turned out clear enough to share around. Lawson remembered the day his father had stuck it in his wallet. The edge got bent because the photo was slightly wider than the plastic holder.

"Come up, please!"

His mind numb, he shoved the wallet into his pocket, closed the phone and climbed wearily to the top of the cliff.

Peta hurried over and, slowly, he pulled out the wallet. She grabbed it and flipped it open.

"It's a picture of you!"

His heart pounded. Cold washed down his back and he pressed his hand to his jaw. "Yes, Dad wouldn't go anywhere without his wallet."

Did this mean that his whole family was gone? Mother, father, brother and his family—all gone? Suddenly, just seeing the wallet, he felt his loss keenly, painfully.

Then another truth hit him.

Danny Culmore had his father's wallet.

Determination flooding through him, he reached across and snatched the wallet from Peta's gentle grasp. He searched it, finding no money, credit cards or any important documents like a driver's license and insurance cards. Only the picture, which was now fading in the damp, salty air.

Tears stung his eyes and he swallowed.

Peta put her arm across his back. She rested her head on his shoulder.

"Talk to me, Lawson."

"It's my father's."

"I'm sorry."

He blinked back tears. "This is my brother." He pointed to his picture. "His wife and their son are also missing."

She made a little sound of sympathy. He rubbed his face, then dropped into a slumped squat on the long grass. It was still damp from last night's fog.

"I think Danny Culmore may have killed them."

Peta's jaw dropped. "Are you sure? Is it his boat down there?"

He nodded. "I saw the registration in the compartment. It listed him as the owner."

The wind had picked up and Peta looked around. "I think another bout of rain is coming in. I was hoping for a nice day."

Yeah, so was he. Even last night as he helped the police inspect the municipal office for damage, all he'd hoped for was warmer weather and some bit of evidence to help Peta. He shoved the wallet into his pocket and stood. "Let's go. While I was down there, I noticed that the tide's turning."

After standing, she gave him a one-armed hug again and released him. "I'm sorry you've lost your family. But do you think that they may be in the witness protection program?"

He shook his head. He'd already ruled that hope out. "I

don't know where my family is, Peta, but I know that, considering the amount of blood found in Marcano's van, my father could never have survived. Still, the DA was reluctant to prosecute anyone because the other evidence was too weak."

She went pensive, then grim. "Do you think Danny was a hit man? And he was forced to kill your family when they accidentally witnessed the murder?"

"Maybe."

"It makes no sense. Why would Danny go all the way down to Boston to kill someone? Surely those who ordered the hit could find a guy to do the job down there. And what would it have to do with his own murder?"

He stared into her eyes, trying to make sense of her words. What was she saying?

She shifted away from him and her sigh was loud. "Lawson," she began, "this is way more complicated than I first thought. With Danny dead, you'll never know the truth. Is that why you've been sticking so close to me? Did you think I had the answers?"

"Peta, I wanted to help you. And, yes, I hoped that you would help me, too. I just wasn't ready for this."

"To be honest, I didn't even expect to find the boat still here. But Danny wasn't one to change habits unless it benefited him big-time." Her brows shot up. "Oh, Lawson, do you think I'm partly to blame for all of this? Because I introduced them?"

When he didn't answer, she looked out toward the old lighthouse, then at the soft clouds dancing at the edge of the horizon. Her expression looked distinctly lost. What could he say to her?

"We should get out of here. We're too exposed. And it's going to rain, again."

Her shoulders dropped. They began to walk toward the

woods, but he stopped them. "Peta," he started again, catching her arm. "I'm sorry. I'd only just met you, and it felt like the break I'd been hoping for."

She swiped her eyes. "It's okay. My past was bound to catch up with me, but I didn't think I'd ever be blamed for something like this. I honestly tried to stop Danny. I practically begged him not to work for Marcano. But it got worse. Danny changed after that. He got ruthless and greedy and wasn't the same happy-go-lucky guy I grew up with."

"Were you still 'trouble' back then?"

"I guess I was. No," she added quickly. "By then, Aunt Linda had died, and I was eighteen and no longer welcome here. I remember Joey Melanson hinting at that. He had helped Doc Garvey with my aunt the night she died, and he told me I should leave." She stiffened. "And he told me that same thing again on the phone."

"Has he always worked for the doctor?"

She flicked up her hands. "All my life, but Joey's old and *not* the smartest person on the island. The odd man out. Before that, he did some fishing, I think, but the rest of the extended family became engineers and such. One uncle was even a scientist. His great-grandfather was one of the lighthouse keepers. They say he designed a more efficient rotating system for it."

Lawson glanced over at the derelict lighthouse, then at the cottage. "So Joey might have a key to the lighthouse. I know I changed the locks on the cottage last week, but hadn't bothered with it."

"It's possible. It was a big family. Half the island's residents can trace their roots to one of the lighthouse keepers, so there could be a dozen keys out there. Why?"

"I wonder if he knows more about what's going on than

we realize. That old drunk had a key to the lighthouse, and I bet he bought his liquor from Danny."

"That old drunk? You mean Benny Melanson?"

"Melanson? Is he Joey's brother?"

"A cousin. But like I said, a lot of people probably have a key. You'll never be able to round them all up."

"Great. What do you know about Benny?"

"He's harmless, really, in case you're thinking he's involved in Danny's death." Her expression seemed bleak. "He's got his troubles, but he's more likely to want to help than anything. He used to be really smart, worked for some company that built highways, and I don't mean he held the caution sign, either. He was really high up in management. Then, he came home and started to drink. Maybe he had a problem before that. I don't know."

She stared at the lighthouse for a moment. "I remember being a schoolkid and having to come up here every spring and clean it up. I hated it. One time I nearly fell off the edge of the cliff."

"That's probably what caused your fear of heights."

She nodded. "Everyone around here was pretty protective of this site. They didn't want it shut down and replaced. I remember my aunt saying that it could have been reconditioned. You could turn it off easily enough, she said."

Lawson looked down at her, feeling his eyebrow twitch. His mind was speeding past his conscious thought too quickly to process everything. The lighthouse. The history.

"Come on." Grabbing her hand, he pulled her down along the trail toward the lighthouse. There, Lawson quickly unlocked the door.

"Phew!" Peta exclaimed. "Close the door for a few minutes and you can barely breathe in here!"

"Benny Melanson broke a bottle of his moonshine in here. I left an upper window open, but it's going to take a few warm days before this smell dissipates."

"At the rate this summer's going, that smell will be here all year. What are you looking for?"

Lawson stooped down behind the narrow staircase that led up to the lights and pulled out a wooden box. When he started to rifle through it, Peta caught his arm. "Let's take it back to the cottage. The smell in here is too strong."

As they walked toward the cottage, the sun dipped behind a cloud, chilling the air. Lawson saw Peta rub her arms, and quickened his steps. The wind had risen since they had been on the path toward Danny's boat.

Inside the kitchen, he dropped the box on the table. Peta put a kettle of water on the stove to boil, and took out a loaf of bread and some peanut butter. Wordlessly, she made some sandwiches, being careful to keep her distance from him, he noticed.

Misery hung heavy on him. He shouldn't be blaming her and a good-size part of him wasn't. She was no more to blame for his parents' disappearance than he was.

The thought pulled him up short. No, he wasn't to blame for their deaths. He'd been late the night they were all supposed to meet. If he hadn't been, he'd be gone, too.

The wind hurled itself against the kitchen window, and rattled a loose eavestrough at the front of the cottage. Somewhere on this island could be his family.

Dead. Buried. Or maybe dumped out in the water.

He'd searched as much of the island as he could.

He hadn't checked the small pond near the path they'd taken last night to escape the gunfire. Could they be there?

Oblivious to his inner thoughts, Peta set a plate of sandwiches down just as the kettle began to whistle. Then she made a big pot of tea. "I know this won't help much, Lawson, but I'm sorry you found that wallet. I wish you'd found something more positive."

Her eyes were kind, sympathetic, understanding in a way that warmed him. "I know. And I'm sorry I even thought that you were responsible. It was just a knee-jerk reaction."

She smiled briefly. "That's okay. Let's see what we can find out here."

Lawson turned his attention to his find. Danny was delving into recent island history, he thought as he set aside the papers and junk that was more than seventy years old.

"What are we looking for?" she asked after covering the teapot with a knitted cozy.

"I don't know. Danny was interested in the island around the Second World War. Maybe this stuff has something that could lead us to what he was searching for."

They sorted through the moldy, crumbling papers, even found a few photographs that Peta picked up.

"This one is Joey—I'm sure of it."

Lawson looked at the old black and white photo. A preteen boy was sitting on the edge of the cliff. "Look at the angle of this thing," he said. "You can even see blurred blades of grass in the foreground. Someone was really low to the ground when this shot was taken."

"Or hanging off the edge of the cliff. Joey doesn't look like he wanted his picture taken. But look at the background. That's this cottage." She walked to the window and peered out. "That photo was taken right where I fell. But you can't hang off a cliff and take a picture at the same time, not with an old camera like the one that must have been used to take this photo."

"Kids can. I hear they take unnecessary risks."

Rolling her eyes, she returned to the kitchen table. Lawson took back the photo and turned it over. The date was 1950. Too late for what he was looking for.

He found an envelope. The handwriting on the front had been in pencil and long since faded. Large and bent, with black mold already rotting one edge, the envelope had become damp at some point and partly sealed itself. Peta, anticipating his need, handed him a knife. He carefully pried it open and spread out the contents.

"What's in it?"

"Schematics of the lighthouse, and what looks like a schedule. No, two schedules."

"Of what?" Peta shifted closer and peered over his arm. He opened the folded papers and studied them for a moment.

He could hear her impatience in her shifting. "That's just an old tide table from 1940! This is the period you want, but I don't think tide times are going to help you."

"They will if they line up with this schedule." He lifted the other paper. "This is a schedule of timings for shutting off the lighthouse light. And look, it's shut off three hours before high tide in each case."

"Why would anyone want to do that? That's the most deadly time."

"And the light stayed off each time for three hours. Wait! Not on all days. Oh, I get it. Only when high tide came after dark."

Peta laughed. "At the worst time, I see. How long did they do it for?"

"A year, it seems. At the height of the war."

Peta poured two cups of tea and, after handing him one, she grabbed a sandwich. "My history is terrible. When was the height of the war? Around 1944?"

"My P.I. friend, Jan, did some digging for me. A lot is on the Net. There is some speculation that German subs came into the mouth of the Bay of Fundy. There's even one report that a submarine officer planted some surveillance equipment along the New Brunswick shore. And there was a rumor that some German sailors came ashore looking for recreation."

"Oh, I don't believe that for a minute! They'd stick out like sore thumbs."

"What if it happened here?"

She sipped her tea, looking surprisingly mild and self-assured. "It wouldn't. This island's too boring and you've already seen how the islanders take to strangers. But you're getting away from the point here. Why would Danny want to know if some German sailors made it to shore sixty-odd years ago? He couldn't possibly have been interested in that."

"I agree. But I know Danny *was* interested in World War II history, the same period during which they shut off the lighthouse light."

"He'd told me he'd found out something. Maybe he was hoping to figure out how to turn off the new light."

Lawson took a sandwich, and ate thoughtfully. "Totally different technology. Do you think you can guess Joey's whereabouts now?"

"Sure. Do you think he'll know why they turned off the lighthouse?" She lowered her teacup for a moment.

"Maybe."

"While we're chatting with him, we'll find out why he felt the need to call me."

He set down the paper he was holding. "You're not coming."

This time her teacup hovered near her lips. "Yes, I am. It was me he called, not you."

"He's dangerous."

"No, he's not. And he won't talk to you. But he'll talk to me."

Lawson frowned in disbelief. "What makes you say that?"

"Because he called me, and he knows me."

"You've been away for ten years."

"It doesn't matter. I was the one who used to defend him when Danny started to torment him."

"I thought you were as bad as Danny."

She shrugged. "Not when it came to Joey. He— I felt sorry for him." With that, she lowered her eyes.

He touched her chin, lifting it. "That's nice, but there's more, isn't there?"

Setting down her tea, she nodded. "He'd told me to leave after my aunt died, but this time, it felt more urgent."

"He could still be dangerous."

"But I don't think he murdered Danny, if that's what you're thinking. Like I said, he'll feel much freer to talk to me than to you, so I have to come with you."

She offered the last sandwich to him. He took it, and bit into it. With a smug smile, she set the plate and her cup into the sink.

"It's raining," he said.

She glanced out the window, then lifted her brows. "You're from Boston, aren't you?"

"Yes, why?"

"And I'm from here. It's just a short cloudburst. We're not going to melt. I have a jacket. Do you?"

"In my Jeep."

She lifted her hands. "Then let's go."

He narrowed his eyes slightly. "Are you sure?"

"Yes. I feel good about this. I've got my alibi intact and we're finally getting somewhere. I hate just sitting around, waiting for things to happen. I want answers. If Joey knows something about Danny's death, we need to know what it is."

"Tell me about this guy. I want to know who we're facing before we pound on his door. And I want to know why you're not scared of him."

Peta took his teacup and set it beside hers in the sink. "Years ago, he had a dog, after he gave up fishing because the fish stocks were depleted. Joey's always been a bit of an outcast. He has an intellectual disability, but he's held down the same job for years now, working for Doc Garvey. He does all kinds of odd jobs for him."

"The dog?" Lawson prompted.

"I was getting to it. Doc Garvey didn't want the dog around the clinic. He said it was unhealthy. The dog was a bit mangy-looking. One day the dog went missing, and Joey was pretty upset."

"The doc had him shot, right?"

"No, but we don't know what exactly happened. The kids at school used to tease Joey, calling him stupider than the dog. That was mostly Danny saying that. He could be cruel. So when Joey came by the school to ask if we'd seen his dog, Danny started in on him. I told him to shut up."

"You didn't tease him, too?"

"No." She pursed her lips before explaining. "Joey had no one. But he had this dog, and the thing loved him. Hey, my aunt wouldn't even let me have a goldfish. I helped him find the dog after school that day. He'd been stuck in Danny's garage. Danny or his parents must have locked him in there by accident."

She stopped talking. He knew, beneath the calm exterior, she was struggling with the memory of not having a single thing to love, while Joey was mocked when his beloved pet had gone missing.

"Later, Danny started to change, working for Gary Marcano. We had a couple of months until graduation and he liked to talk about how he was going to make a ton of money, thanks to Gary. Around the same time, Joey told me to leave."

"And that was the last time you talked to him?"

She shook her head. "No. Remember, my aunt died shortly afterward—Joey was helping with the body. Doc Garvey used to get him to do stuff in the morgue next to the clinic. Joey stood beside me when I went to see my aunt. He told me she was dead for sure."

"For sure?"

"He thought that was why I went in to see her. He also told me to leave the island and not look back."

"Doesn't sound like a friend talking."

"Believe me, it was. Joey never condemned me, even before I found his dog. A kindred spirit, maybe. I just know that his advice was the best anyone could give me. I left shortly after that."

"I still don't like your coming with me to see him."

"But he won't talk to you, so you have no choice."

"That call could be considered a threat."

She stopped as she was slipping on her jacket. "True, but I don't think it was."

"You said he was intellectually disabled. Could he also be mentally ill?"

She shrugged. "I don't think so. Wouldn't Doc Garvey have noticed that? He wouldn't want a mentally ill man working in the medical clinic, even if it was just to clean and do odd jobs."

Lawson had no answer for that. All he knew was that when they did meet Joey Melanson face-to-face, he was going to make sure he stood between Peta and the guy.

* * *

Peta shivered. The rain had finished but not before the fog rolled in. Only in the Maritimes did you see two lousy weather conditions like fog and rain at the same time.

Joey Melanson had warned her to leave ten years ago. Three days ago, he'd told her she shouldn't have come back. Why?

It was unlikely that it had anything to do with Danny's death, but how could she know for sure? Was Lawson's concern for her safety justified?

Was it even welcome?

The way her heart was pounding proved that it was. But she'd have to be crazy to take his concern as a sign of something larger. He was here to find answers to his own troubles. Just because their goals overlapped didn't mean he was ready for any personal commitment.

Did that mean that she was?

She threw on her coat and tugged the door open. Glancing back at Lawson, she hurried out of the cottage. Lawson followed, and after waiting for him to leave, she locked the door. She was glad he'd brought his Jeep. Judging by the dark bank of clouds beyond the coast of Maine, they were in for more short, intense downpours.

Close to where she'd fallen, the road dipped. The ground, supersaturated, could no longer absorb the water, and they pushed through a large puddle.

"More erosion," Peta murmured as muddy water flew away from the Jeep.

"If the ground wasn't so soft, I'd have gone around it. The driveway seemed a lot more bumpy when we first came in here."

Peta gripped the dash, forcing herself not to look out her window. They were far too close to the cliff.

They rounded the bend in the driveway, plunging into the

woods just as the clouds opened. Lawson had already flicked on the wipers. With the branches now slashing in the rising wind, they were in for another messy evening.

"Joey's house has always been that one, right behind the clinic." Peta pointed to the small bungalow diagonally across from the cottage driveway. It was mere feet from the clinic, and indeed, feet from them, but with the driving rain, Lawson decided to turn into the back parking lot of the clinic. Fortunately, the clinic and Joey's small house sat on the corner where the road bent.

"He's outside!" Peta pressed forward against her seat belt, straining to see through the windshield. Lawson pulled closer to the house. His headlights were nearly useless, but they caught the older man waving his arms wildly.

Lawson climbed out, leaving the Jeep running. The rain rushed in on a gust of wind, spraying Peta. Over the sounds of the rain and the engine, she heard Lawson yell, "What's wrong?"

"Ground's too soft. Go back!" Joey answered.

Peta threw open the passenger door. Something in the old man's tone, the kind of urgency she'd heard on the phone snagged her to attention.

He hurried over to them. "Too much water. You should park in front of the clinic."

"It's all right. I have four-wheel drive," Lawson assured him.

Peta wiped her face. "Can we talk to you, Joey? About the lighthouse?"

He screwed up his face and blinked back the rain slashing at his face. "The lighthouse? Why? Because of Benny? You aren't dumb like me, Peta. You know Benny won't hurt you. Just go, like I told you before."

"Let's talk inside, Joey, please. We're getting soaked," Peta called back over the rain and wind.

Joey threw off his hood, and the rain beat down on his thinning gray hair, plastering it to his forehead in seconds. "Don't say bad things about Benny. He's good, better than other people around here. He cares about people. You gotta leave him alone."

Peta glanced at Lawson, then back at Joey. "We're not here about Benny, but do you know where he was getting his liquor?"

"In the States. Benny helped Danny so he could earn the stuff. Danny should have paid him money, not liquor. Liquor's bad for Benny."

Lawson leaned in to speak in her ear. "I don't think we're going to get much out of him in this rain."

She shook her head. "Wait a sec. Joey, what work was Benny doing for Danny?"

Joey shook his head. "I'm not supposed to gossip. The pastor said so." He spun his heel in the soft grass, but his balance wavered for a moment as he seemed to get his foot stuck in the sodden earth. Lawson stepped up to him, but the old man shook his head and held up his hand as he hurried toward his house.

"Go away! It ain't safe here." Then with a look of horror on his face, he dropped out of sight.

Literally, as if the ground itself had swallowed him up.

He was gone before Peta even had a chance to gasp.

TEN

"No!" Peta rushed forward, not believing her eyes. But she'd taken only a few steps when Lawson spun around and grabbed her.

"Peta, don't move!" His arms wrapped around her and dragged her down to the soaking earth.

She leaned over his shoulder, straining to peer through the rain. "What happened? He's disappeared into thin air!"

"No, he hasn't. It's a sinkhole. The ground under him has collapsed." He scanned the area. "We have to get out of here. It's not safe."

"But we can't leave Joey!"

"I don't plan to. Start crawling toward the road. Don't get into the Jeep. Go to the church, or the parsonage beside it and get help."

"What about you?"

"I'll pull Joey out. He probably hasn't fallen in too far. But the whole area could be unstable."

She hesitated. Lawson caught her face between his hands. The rain and wind couldn't obscure the deep concern etched on his features. He blinked away the water running down his forehead. "Please, Peta. Every second is crucial. Go get help."

He stretched closer and kissed her firmly on the mouth. The kiss was over before she realized it. "And pray, too."

Then, he gently pushed her on her way.

"A sinkhole?" Peta asked. "I've never heard of one here. I thought they were only in Florida."

They were sitting once again at the clinic. Thankfully, Lawson had managed to pull Joey out, though how, she had no idea. Joey was no lightweight.

"It's from the caves underneath," Joey said, still rubbing his shoulder as he tried to get comfortable on a chair in the waiting room.

Caves? Sure, there were a few minor indents in the cliffs, but even the local kids weren't stupid enough to venture into them. The incoming tide could turn one into a death trap in a matter of minutes.

"There aren't any caves here," growled Doctor Garvey, looking up from the report he was filling out at the counter. "It's just because we've had a wet spring. That area had some soft fill put in years ago. It's finally settled."

Peta glanced over at Lawson. His clothes were still soaked, and he remained standing on the industrial mat by the door, trying to brush off the excess water. Their eyes met, and for a moment, he looked regretful. Why? she wondered.

Then, she remembered the wallet. Her heart twisted. Lawson hadn't even had time to sort that pain out yet.

"There aren't any caves here," Doc Garvey repeated. "This island isn't like the mainland. Different rock. Too hard."

"There's an indent by the cove," she corrected.

"That's just an indent. Besides, it wouldn't go in far enough to cause a sinkhole behind the clinic."

That was true. The distance was almost a mile. As the crow flies, where she had fallen was the closest water to them.

Could it be just the land settling? She hadn't had a chance to talk to Lawson since he hurried her down to get the pastor. There at the parsonage, the pastor's wife called 911. But by the time Peta had returned with the pastor, Lawson had already pulled Joey to safety.

But still, it seemed an odd coincidence that Joey would be swallowed up in that area right at that moment. *What does this mean, Lord?*

"Well, we've taped it off. When it stops raining, or in the morning, we'll have a look," Long stated, accepting the doctor's report. Another officer, one from the mainland, was helping Joey with yet another report.

Peta wanted to ask about the gunshots last night, but held back. Hardly the best time.

"The hole is dangerous," Joey said. "Too many people have been hurt lately."

Doc Garvey tossed down his pen. "Only you got hurt, and this hasn't got anything to do with the murder." He threw Peta a sharp look. She thought about when she first arrived. Had Doc Garvey told the police anything? Head downcast, and a red stain creeping up his neck, Joey stood. "My house ain't safe. It's too close to the hole."

"Honestly," the doctor snapped back. "If you feel that scared, stay behind the clinic. You've done it before and you have to be there first thing in the morning, anyway."

Peta lifted her brows. Wasn't that where the morgue was? No, wait, there was also a tiny apartment, too. It was just a kitchenette, bathroom and a closet-size bedroom, if she remembered correctly.

Joey turned to Peta. "Why did you come to see me? Were you sick again?"

"Never mind her," the doctor answered. "You've finished your report to the police. Get some rest. If Peta needs something, I'll help her."

Rubbing his shoulder, Joey shuffled into the rear apartment. The wind had died down, and the rain had eased off, thankfully, but by now, a heavy dusk had settled. Again, Lawson's pensive gaze connected with hers, obviously not happy at the way things were turning out.

Peta stared back at him. His expression mirrored her own feelings about the doctor's treatment of Joey. And oddly, a warmth rippled within her.

"Do you want to go home?" he asked her.

She would have liked to talk to Joey, regardless of what Doc Garvey wanted. Joey may be staying at the clinic, and the clinic may belong to Doc Garvey, but the man could talk to anyone he wanted to. Yet, maybe it was best to let them all sleep on it. She nodded.

Lawson took her back to the cottage. They slowed as they passed the hole, now encircled with yellow crime-scene tape. She turned to Lawson. "How deep is it?"

"Hard to say. It was still collapsing as I was helping Joey out. But at least ten feet."

She bit her lip. "Kind of deep for a bit of settling land."

"Do you remember when they put the fill in, or was that after you left?"

Sadly, she shook her head. "It must have been before I came along. I don't remember it at all. But I do remember when Joey's little house was built."

"What was there before?"

"Nothing. Just a garden, I think. Joey lived at the back of

the clinic before it was renovated, and used to grow a few vegetables where the hole and the house are now."

"The fill might have been put there for the garden." Lawson eased his vehicle forward. They crossed the road and Peta held her breath as they slipped into the woods again. Was the rain going to erode even more of the land? Near the cliff, maybe?

She held her breath. "I can't help but wonder if we're going to find more sinkholes."

He rolled past the cliff and stopped by the cottage before speaking. She unbuckled her seat belt as he asked, "How many caves are there here?"

"Only the one you found. The rocks here aren't really cave material. Doc Garvey's right. Any indents don't go in deep. They weren't even worth hanging out in, and teenagers would take anything that's available to drink in. More likely, we'd use the old herring smokehouses at the other end of the island." She shook her head. "Still, I don't think the hole is just from some settling soil. I can't explain why, but it's too much of a coincidence."

"I agree." He paused. "Joey Melanson knows something about the lighthouse, and local history, and things Danny was looking into. Then right when we were going to speak to him, he nearly loses his life? To me, that's suspicious."

"Mind you, there are easier ways to silence a guy. Look at the way Doc Garvey has to just tell him off and Joey shuts up."

Lawson eyed her. "Do you think that Danny was shut up?"

"I don't know." She leaned forward, and touched his arm. "Lawson, it hurts me terribly to know that I introduced Danny to Gary, and that they could have been involved in your family's disappearance."

He leaned back, inhaling deeply. "At the clinic, I had some

time to think. It was unfair of me to blame you. All I've wanted to do this past year is find my family, hopefully alive, and bring whoever is responsible to justice. So what Gary and Danny did after you introduced them is hardly your fault."

"I can't help but feel as though I set everything bad in motion."

"Well, don't. You carry around enough guilt." He gathered her into his arms, scrunching the hair at the back of her head gently and then letting it go. She leaned into him, hating how grateful she felt for his touch. Shame for all she'd done washed over her, and yet, she wanted to ignore it. She also wanted to ignore the reason Lawson was here—to exact justice for his family. Now that Danny was dead, Lawson would never find the closure he needed.

Lawson drew in his breath, preparing to speak. "Don't feel sorry. We… Maybe we should let it go."

She shut her eyes. "Something that can't be done here, I'm afraid. I mean, how can I let it all go, when looking around, I see the café I vandalized, the grocery store I used to hang out behind, doing things I shouldn't have, and…" She thought of the house she'd grown up in, the one two doors down from Danny's which, she heard, had burned to the ground a few years back. At least she hadn't done that.

She thought of Aunt Kathleen. Kathleen hadn't even talked to her yet. But then again, she hadn't made any effort at reconciliation, either.

Did that mean it was time?

Lawson's hand fell to her shoulder, as if its heavy weight was trying to pin her down, keep her here on the island. "Don't be thinking you can't let go of your past. Isn't there something to be said for desensitization? Like getting a person who's afraid to fly up a few times in an airplane so that the fear can be eased somehow?"

"Are you afraid of flying?" she asked.

"No. But I was always scared of snakes. So my father took me to a reptile exhibit at the zoo. Every day after school while it was there, until I could even hold the one they used for demonstrations. The whole zoo knew us by name by the time the exhibit was done."

She smiled at him. "Come on, let's go talk to Joey. I'm sure he'll talk to me, even if Doc Garvey has told him not to." With that, she twisted around to buckle up again.

Lawson opened the Jeep's door. "Not tonight, I'm afraid. We all need some decent rest." He climbed out, and walked around to her door, opening it for her.

She climbed out.

"Is your cell phone charged?"

"Yes."

"I'll call you and I'll even take you out for breakfast tomorrow morning. How's seven? We'll talk to Joey then, before Doc Garvey gets in."

"Good idea." She wet her lips. "If the café will serve me, that is."

Lawson smiled, but his smile had a grim edge to it. "They will."

She forced out a grin. He stepped closer. "Peta, God can help you deal with the mistakes you've made. All He wants us to do is to take that first step. Remember the prodigal son, and his return to his father?"

"Of course. Why?"

"His father watched and waited each day for his son to return."

"That's nice, but, Lawson, I'm not a prodigal anymore. I gave my life to Jesus a long time ago."

"You gave your future to Him, Peta. But you didn't give Him your past."

She didn't answer.

"Peta, it's one thing to remember what you did, so that you don't do it again, but it's another to keep it locked inside you as punishment. Do you understand the difference?"

She blinked. At that moment, he leaned forward and kissed her mouth. His lips lingered, and she shut her eyes.

Then he pulled back and returned to his Jeep.

Lawson knew Peta would be waiting for him. When he knocked at ten to seven the next morning, she opened the kitchen door almost immediately, her cheerfulness a bit forced, but the effort was there. "I'm almost ready."

He stepped into the kitchen. The first question he wanted to ask her was if she'd prayed about what he'd said last night. She had a lot of baggage that the Lord could easily unload. All it would take was prayer.

But are you the one to tell her what to do?

Certainly not, he answered himself, feeling the corner of his father's wallet dig into his chest. He'd come for justice, driven by anger and pain. When he'd arrived on Northwind, he'd wanted to kill Danny immediately, even though, at that time, he was harboring nothing more than some vague suspicions. It had been the pastor here who'd helped him temper his hostility. But while he learned to bide his time, the desire for revenge had still seethed within him.

Now what was he doing? Still holding on to his father's wallet, still trying to sort out his feelings.

The story of the prodigal son he'd mentioned last night returned to him. In a way, he was the prodigal's brother, full of self-righteous anger.

"Let's go. I'm hungry," he said with straightened shoulders. "I've lived on granola bars and coffee for the last day. Trudy brought in some pastries from her café, but the cops all got to them before me."

"Trudy's a good cook. I've missed her signature dishes."

After they climbed into his Jeep, he turned to her. "When I was driving in this morning, I noticed the hole was already filled in."

Her face showed surprise. "By whom?"

He shrugged. "I'd say Doc Garvey ordered it filled in. He was probably concerned that it would erode further."

"That was quick. Joey must be glad, I'm sure."

He still didn't want her speaking with Joey. But the old man seemed like less of a threat this morning. And though she might be better able to coax information out of him, based on their shared history, Lawson had also earned his trust by pulling the older man to safety from the sinkhole.

The morning had started bright and sunny and, of course, the wind was picking up. Halfway there, Peta spoke. "Joey's intellectually challenged. He's always been like that. I don't know if he has a specific disorder or if he's even been tested. They didn't do too much of that years ago. But it's important to know how to talk to him."

"How?"

"You need to ask him simple, direct, nonthreatening questions. Sometimes, Joey sounds normal, and sounds like he's following along with the conversation, but he struggles with big words and people who look down on him. And he gets flustered easily."

"So we should just keep it simple, stay calm?"

"Exactly. We may need to repeat some questions. Joey's logic is a bit skewed, and I think Benny's may be, too. Some people used to say it was genetic, but I think Benny's may be from years of alcohol abuse. Neither of them think the same way normal people think, so don't assume that Joey will be able to follow our train of thought." She stopped and turned to him. "Joey isn't bad. He can be confused, but I honestly think he doesn't want to hurt anyone."

Her belief. Lawson would decide for himself.

A few minutes later, they were seated at the café, at the back where they'd been before. Ellie came out, her expression so guarded it nearly made Lawson smile. She handed them menus, and when she left, his suppressed smile broke free into a wide grin.

"Yes," Peta said quietly when scanning the menu, "I know. I know. Ellie's been told to serve us. But she doesn't want to."

"And we shouldn't say anything?"

She studied the menu. "And you shouldn't smile, either."

"I can't help it."

She peeked over the top of her menu. Her eyes sparkled, and he knew she was smiling. Despite all that had happened, he found himself warming inside. "What will you have?"

"The breakfast casserole looks good. Eggs, ham and spinach."

Ellie returned and Lawson ordered two casseroles, both with whole-wheat toast and coffee and juice. After taking back the menus, the waitress huffed off.

Peta looked around, while Lawson watched her. If they'd met in Toronto, or Boston, or under any normal circumstances, like at church, would they have shown each other any interest? His mother used to extol the wonder of falling in love, of that one person put on the earth for just you, the perfect mate to help you grow in Christ.

But would that have happened under any other circumstances?

"Look at this," Peta interrupted his thoughts. She'd swiveled around to stare at the wall behind her.

"What is it?"

"An old newspaper article. Northwind's *Weekly News* has been publishing for about a century. This one's from the forties."

Interested, he stood. Until recently, he hadn't known of Danny's interest in history. He'd been watching Danny for months, biding his time, waiting for him to slip up, and reveal where Lawson's family might be. But since this new information on him, Lawson hadn't considered checking the *Weekly News*' archives.

He leaned forward and quietly read the framed article.

IS NORTHWIND READY FOR AN ATTACK?

While there is heavy fighting overseas, those of us back home may see some of it ourselves. In a report released by the Navy last week, in conjunction with a similar report released by the U.S. War Department, officials stated that they are worried that enemy submarines have already slipped into North American waters.

So what are we on the homefront to do? "Keep vigilant," one officer interviewed said. "We have plans in place for such events."

With Northwind so isolated and at the entrance to the Bay of Fundy, will we see the enemy up close? Some locals aren't worried, saying that the treacherous waters and our small size make us an unlikely target. Others interviewed remind everyone that Halifax, facing the Atlantic and hundreds of miles from here, has more reason to be worried.

But local council members agree with the advice of being vigilant, adding that we do our part in the war effort by being watchful, and always remembering that "loose lips sink ships."

"Here's another one," Peta said, pointing to a smaller article at the next table. This early in the morning, they were the only ones in the café.

Lawson scanned it quickly. It was dated two months later. A submarine had been spotted in the Gulf of Maine, but again, as in the earlier article, local council members sounded calm, unconcerned almost. Strangely, the reporter who penned the article didn't press for a reason.

Peta had begun to scan the other framed clippings. Lawson could see one about Old Sow, and another about the lighthouse, and its importance to small watercraft and fishing boats. Without the light, small boats could get dragged around the southeast corner of the island. Treacherous rocks, lying just below the surface on that side, would spell disaster.

Another talked about a visiting soldier, credited with saving the life of a small child who'd fallen through the ice on the very pond Lawson had not searched.

Behind him, Peta gasped. He turned, expecting her to have made some connection that he hadn't yet made.

But she was staring out the bay window. He followed her gaze. Coming into the café was Kathleen McPherson.

The woman's sharp stare cut through the pretty pale blue–curtained window, right at Peta. He could tell she was holding her breath.

The woman entered the café. For someone in her eighties, she was fairly spry, with curly salt-and-pepper hair and a crisp, clean summer pantsuit. But the glare on her features stole any youthfulness that may have remained.

Peta stiffened as the woman shut the door.

"Hello, Aunt Kathleen. How are you?"

"I've been better. This whole island has been better. Trouble didn't start until you came back."

Peta pressed her lips together. She was holding herself so tight that Lawson was sure she'd snap apart at any moment.

He turned to the woman. "I'd say the trouble started before she came. With Danny's death."

"His murder. She murdered him."

"I did not!"

Lawson folded his arms. He wanted to respect this older woman, as he'd been taught to do all his life, but it was hard with her condemning attitude. "That may have been the assumption, but you'll find that Peta has a solid alibi."

The woman had trouble holding in her surprise. "She has?"

Ellie came out of the kitchen, holding a small paper bag, obviously a take-out item that Kathleen had ordered. The waitress stopped between Kathleen and Peta.

Ignoring Ellie, the older woman peered hard at them. "Still, look what else has happened. Random shootings, bump in the bedrock. People breaking into houses. It all started when she came."

"If that rumbling was a geological bump," Peta reasoned, "I think it did a good thing and exposed that sinkhole before it did any real damage."

The older woman sniffed and Lawson caught a family resemblance in the gray eyes and short nose.

Peta stepped forward. "Aunt Kathleen, I didn't kill anyone. I discovered Danny dead, that's all. And I know you don't want me here, but this was my home, too. The only home I ever had, even if it wasn't the most loving. I'm sorry you can't just give me that much. I mean, I didn't get much from Mum, or Linda. So I guess I can't expect much from you, even at your age."

Kathleen blinked, snatched the take-out bag and muttered, "We've all had it hard here, Peta. Some of us weren't made to be parents, and your mother and Linda were in that category. And all I ever wanted was to keep your uncle's family business safe. Safe from things that could ruin this whole place, like you and Danny."

With that, she hurried out of the café. Peta began to follow her, but stopped at the door. Lawson watched as Kathleen threw one last glance over her shoulder, a stubborn, tight-lipped look that, strangely, showed vulnerability around the eyes.

"You're food's almost ready," Ellie said abruptly.

Peta jumped. Lawson led her back to their table. After Ellie returned to the kitchen, Peta said, "Aunt Kathleen was never able to have children. I hadn't realized that it bothered her, but I think it did. And still does."

"She should have adopted you instead of your aunt Linda taking you in."

"I think Aunt Kathleen wanted her own children, not her baby sister's castoffs. My mother tended to be spoiled, and I wonder if that didn't ruin her ability to raise me. She never fully matured."

"Where is she?"

"She died a few years back." Her eyes glazed over. Did it still, after all these years, bother her that her mother had discarded her? "Her boyfriend at the time didn't even bother to bury her. He just up and left, and the police tracked me down. She'd been living in Halifax, so I buried her there."

"I'm sorry."

"I'm sorry, too. She wasn't very happy."

By then, Ellie had arrived with their meals. They dug into them, and though Lawson knew that Peta's mind was on her family, he knew they needed to talk about what had been happening between them.

"These framed clippings on the walls have got me thinking. The residents here during the war were very tight-lipped."

Several people, policemen included, entered the café and sat by the window. Peta lowered her eyes, and her voice. "Like they are now?"

"I mean, even the reporter writing the story wasn't too concerned about the fact that enemy subs could have been lurking just offshore."

She set her toast down. "You read the article about the hidden rocks. A sub would have to be crazy to venture close to the island."

"What if the reporter had another reason to seem unconcerned?"

"What do you mean?" She lit up and set down her fork. "You mean, if he knew about the dangerous waters at high tide, and how a sub could hit a rock?"

"'Loose lips sink ships.'"

She smiled. "I understand. And that's why the lighthouse was turned off just before high tide. It was put there to warn about the currents. A sub in these waters would have to ride close to the surface, because it's not deep here. Normally, it would see the lighthouse and avoid the island. But if it didn't see the lighthouse, it could get caught in the currents and grounded on the rocks."

Lawson finished his toast before speaking. "I was thinking that the likelihood of a sub coming here must have been small, for the people here not to be concerned, but if they had a plan in place to trap a sub…"

Peta continued to eat. "Then they wouldn't be concerned. But what kind of plan?"

"An ambush."

Her eyes wide, Peta swallowed. "Someone would have been waiting for them? I suppose there could have been members of the militia there. Someone not fit for fighting overseas, or too old. Do you think they may have stayed in the lighthouse? That's where you found all that historical stuff."

"I don't think so. It's too far up from the water." Lawson glanced over at the tables by the front window. Three were already filled up with strangers. "That stuff was only pertinent to the lighthouse, which really doesn't have a good view of small boats after they turn the corner of the island. Maybe at the wharf? It's the next thing you see."

"Too far. It's over a mile from the corner." She stopped, her mouth open and her eyes distant. "As kids, we were always warned not to go near the cliffs. They were dangerous, we were told, but what if there was another reason they didn't want us down there?"

"A cave?"

"Yes, a natural redoubt? A fortress inside the cliff, and the military occupied it. It could contain some ammunition, even. And Joey mentioned a cave."

"There's one small article over by the window that mentions a visiting soldier saving the life of a child."

Peta glanced toward the window. "I missed that. Most of the other articles just talk about good news events." She took another thoughtful bite. "You know, if the military abandoned a cave here, of course we kids would be warned to stay away. Who knows what they would have left, especially if they were hoping to fire upon enemy subs."

"True, and I was also thinking about the soldier. His name isn't mentioned, just his occupation, which is odd

because if he was from Northwind, he'd have been mentioned. So what was he doing here, except something for
the military?"

"You're thinking that he was here on duty? And my
mother's generation would have been told the same thing us
kids were told? It's our grandparents' generation who would
probably have known the truth. Heard it from adults during
World War II. But loose lips sink ships."

"Do you think Danny would have gone looking for a cave?"

She shook her head. "He didn't bother with the cliffs when
he was a kid."

"Well, I think somebody tipped him off to the possibility
of a cave. That's why he was searching wartime history.
Maybe Doc Garvey's mistaken about the type of rock here.
There could be a cave."

"But knowing about the existence of a cave once used to
stockpile weapons isn't enough to kill a person, or go after
me."

"But an offshore bank account that could be worth a lot
might be, and with friends like Gary Marcano, Danny could
have been planning an escape. Or something against Marcano,
using the cave."

She set down her fork, then picked it up, only to set it down
again. Obviously, she was deep in thought. "Do you think
Gary killed him? Danny may have been blackmailing him. He
was capable of that." Their big breakfasts nearly done, she
pushed her plate away. "We need to talk to Joey. I have a
feeling he knows a lot about this cave. He's very protective
and secretive, and certainly old enough to remember firsthand
stories about the war. We should talk to him."

Lawson dug out his cell phone and from the programmed
phone book, found the clinic's number. He dialed it.

But Doc Garvey answered and, when Lawson asked for Joey, the doctor bluntly told him that Joey hadn't shown up for work that morning.

"I wonder where he is," Peta said after Lawson told her. "Do you think he could have gone to the cottage, knowing that we wanted to talk to him?"

"Let's go find out."

They paid the bill and hurried past the group of police officers who'd decided to enjoy a well-deserved breakfast. None of them looked refreshed. Too much happening around here. The shooting, called random by the police; according to the radio, an earthquake or a bump that could have caused the ground to give way, forming a sinkhole; and the murder—all were keeping law enforcement busy.

A few minutes later, they were just reaching the end of the woods with the cottage ahead. Lawson was about to turn the Jeep to the right, when a flash of movement caught his eye. Immediately, he stopped.

Through the few trees left in front of them, and across the field, he could see someone disappearing around the front of the cottage.

ELEVEN

It was a woman, Lawson noticed, and she was carrying a large duffel bag, on which was embroidered the brilliant and recognizable symbol of a local TV station.

She was the reporter they'd seen at the café when Ellie refused to serve them.

"What's wrong?"

"You have a guest."

Peta stared through the trees. "I don't see anyone."

"She just turned the corner. A reporter." He tapped his fingers on his steering wheel. "And I don't know about you, but I don't feel like talking to the media right now."

Peta stiffened. "I haven't done anything wrong."

He put the Jeep into Reverse, and swung his arm around the back of Peta's seat. After he'd guided it back through the woods, he added, "For a troublemaker who got her boyfriend involved in drugs, and who has lived in Toronto for the last ten years, you are remarkably naive."

"Well, gee, thank you," she answered tartly. "I really haven't had much experience with murder, even living in Toronto. I'm sorry if I appear naive to you, but when I gave my life to the Lord, I let go of my old self."

Lawson swung his Jeep onto the road, and shoved the gear-shift into Drive before looking at her. "Did you, Peta? If you had really let go of it, would you have come back here?"

Folding her arms, she didn't answer.

"Maybe you did because the guilt that haunts you brought you back." He softened. "And returning here, with your past, has made you believe that you were always the worst one here. But that's not the case now. Now someone is worse than you, Peta. Someone is a murderer."

He offered her a grim smile. "Maybe that's why you seem naive to me."

Her eyes watered. Then, blinking away the tears, she shot him a calm look. "I *have* considered calling a lawyer, but with everything that's happened, I haven't been able to find the time." She glanced over her right shoulder at the woods. "I do agree with you on one thing, though. I don't want to talk to anyone, much less a reporter."

Lawson remembered when she'd stood in front of the bed-and-breakfast, and how she had winced at Constable Long's mention of her past and how Aunt Kathleen had whipped the NO VACANCY sign up pretty quick. If Peta didn't want the local police to mention her past publicly, she certainly wouldn't want a reporter questioning it.

And he had no desire to tell a reporter what had brought *him* to the island.

Maybe he should take his own advice and get himself a lawyer, too.

They ended up at Lawson's house, trepidation still waffling through Peta. She hadn't seen anyone at the cottage, but Lawson had seen the TV station's logo.

Someone from the media. Mercy, she had no desire to talk

to anyone about Danny's death. Not if she were as naive as Lawson thought she was.

Was she?

As soon as she'd landed in Toronto, she'd found a home church, and then a job. She'd been the bad kid on Northwind, but it didn't compare with the rest of the world. She knew that. T.O. was big and as dangerous as any city, but she'd plunged herself into her work and studying her new faith, and refusing to go near those who could destroy her fragile new start on life.

She shut her eyes. Mercy, she *was* naive.

As Lawson swung into the driveway and killed the engine, she wondered how she could have become this way.

Was it because of her guilt? Feeling so guilty about how she'd acted years ago could make it seem like she was foolishly innocent now, thinking that all these people were justified in not wanting her here or trusting her. Had that created some resemblance to naiveté?

Regardless, she'd better shed it quickly. Someone on this island wasn't justified in wanting her gone.

And that someone was a murderer.

Slowly, she unbuckled her seat belt and slipped from the Jeep. Lawson caught her concern across the hood and frowned, leaving her feeling even more foolish. She ducked her head down. They both reached the corner of the house when Lawson stopped. Still staring at her feet, Peta plowed into him.

A man was standing at the door, his knuckles raised as if to rap on it.

Peta felt Lawson's hand pushing her securely behind him. "Can I help you?"

The man lowered his hand and trotted down the few wooden steps toward them. Lawson's palm remained firmly on Peta's waist, keeping her close behind him.

"I'm James Daley, from Channel 5 news. Can you spare a few minutes?"

"Not really."

"You're Lawson Mills, aren't you?"

"Perhaps."

"And you're renting the lighthouse cottage, too? The one where this woman—" he indicated Peta behind Lawson "—is currently staying? May I ask you a few questions concerning the death of Danny Culmore?"

"I don't know anything more than you do, I'm afraid."

Undaunted, the man peered past Lawson. "Miss Donald, don't the police consider you the prime suspect in Danny Culmore's murder? Do you have anything to say about that?"

Peta pushed Lawson's hand away and stepped forward boldly. "Just that his death is regrettable, but I don't have any knowledge of who might have murdered him."

"Then you don't know that Joey Melanson is accused of drugging the man?"

She gasped. "Where did you hear that?"

"We received a tip that he drugged Danny so that his cousin Benny could murder him."

"Why would Benny want Danny dead?"

"Because Danny was his main supplier of illegal liquor and Danny had decided to cut him off."

Peta frowned. Was that true? But Benny, having been an alcoholic for longer than she'd been alive, always had money for liquor. Unless Danny no longer had work for him, and therefore refused to give him any liquor?

Lawson grabbed her arm. "Well, it seems you know more than we do, so there's no point in this interview, is there?"

"Or is Joey Melanson covering for you, Miss Donald?" the

reporter asked as they slipped past him. "After all, he'd met with you a few nights ago, hadn't he?"

Peta turned, yanking her arm out of Lawson's grip. Forget naiveté. She had the truth. "I was sick that night and Joey let me into the clinic. It's his job."

"Is that really his job? He's just a custodian, not a nurse, and being let into the clinic that carries the drugs that were found in Danny's system would appear to be suspicious to the police, wouldn't it? I mean, Joey isn't really allowed to let people in."

But the nurse had the night off, Peta remembered Joey saying. She shot the reporter a scathing look. "How do you know what drugs, if any, were found in Danny's system?"

The reporter reddened. "Do you know the results of the tox report, yet, Miss Donald? Is there any reason you should even consider that drugs were involved?"

"We have no comment," Lawson gritted out, dragging Peta into his house. She wanted so badly to shout out what she knew, but Lawson propelled her into his kitchen before returning to the door and throwing the lock.

"He was goading you, Peta," Lawson growled as he returned to the kitchen. "Couldn't you see that?"

She peeled off her jacket. "But what he said about Joey—"

"Is completely untrue. First up, Joey wouldn't have access to the drug cabinet, and the drug found in your bottle and probably in Danny's system certainly wouldn't be found in a medical clinic because they're illegal in Canada."

"I knew that. If you'd let me say that—"

Lawson kept talking. "And it's unlikely that Joey and Benny would have killed Benny's main supplier."

"What if Danny had refused to sell him any more liquor?"

"In the first place, we have no proof that Danny *was* the local rumrunner, and second, was there any indication that

Danny had suddenly decided to do what's right, and get out of the business, if he was in it at all?"

Peta pursed her lips and felt her shoulders drop. "None, I'd say. I guess that reporter was just rattling my chain. By throwing out that bone of speculation, he was probably hoping I'd admit something newsworthy. You know, I've seen him do some news reports that have made it all the way to the national news. He seemed so nice."

"Reporters can be nice, but they have a job to do, first and foremost. And that sometimes makes them underhanded."

She found a seat at the dining table, and shoved away the messy piles of papers strewn about. Lawson gathered them up, taking some time to separate a few from the main pile to place on the nearby desk.

"Joey could have stolen the keys to the drug cabinet," she offered quietly.

"Does he strike you as that kind of person? And does Doc Garvey look like the kind of person who'd take a chance and leave the keys unguarded?"

"No, but Joey is the kind of man who protects those he loves."

"Are you saying he's protecting you? First up, he would have had to know that you were coming here, and what would he have been protecting you from?" Lawson asked.

"Not me, but Benny, who is his only family now."

"Protect him from what?"

"Maybe not protect him so much as do something for him." She brightened. "Maybe he killed Danny because he *was* Benny's liquor supplier. This way, Benny wouldn't drink himself into an early grave."

"Early? The guy is over eighty and still going strong," Lawson said. "Your theory is good, but you didn't see the supply of liquor Benny had stashed away in the lighthouse.

If Danny was the local rumrunner, then he stocked Benny up pretty good. Besides, we don't have any proof of any of that. And what about Marcano?"

She shrugged. "I don't know. I'm just throwing out ideas. You know, eliminate the impossible and whatever remains must be true."

He pulled out a chair beside her and sat down. "You've watched too many Sherlock Holmes movies. Besides, I think Danny's death has something to do with his behavior and his interest in World War II history."

"What makes you think that?"

"Because Danny Culmore was involved with Gary Marcano. Because of what happened to my family, I've learned how to investigate. Most of the time, circumstantial evidence is just as important and can lead you to the truth as easily as solid proof like my father's wallet."

"So when Danny told me he wasn't involved with Gary Marcano anymore, he was lying to me." She held up her hand. "Before you say anything, I know people lie. In my job, I deal with Workers' Compensation claims, and yes, some people lie about their injuries. I just didn't expect it from Danny. There was no reason for him to lie to me."

"Maybe he thought that if you knew he was still involved with Gary, you wouldn't come."

She shrugged. "Yes, but there doesn't seem to have been a party planned at all. So it looks like he lied twice. Except that not planning is—was—so much like Danny, so maybe that means nothing at all. And inviting me was just Danny being spontaneous. It's as if he'd asked me to come because he knew he was going to die and wanted to say goodbye. Crazy, isn't it?"

"So he could be spontaneous?"

"Yes."

Abruptly, a merry little song danced through the air. Lawson's cell phone was ringing. He pulled a face as he stood and walked into the living room. Feeling a bit awkward, Peta rose and walked to the back door they'd just entered. Cautiously, she peeked out. No sign of the reporter.

There had been two reporters at the café, a man and a woman. Had they split up to cover more territory? Knowing the islanders, they weren't going to get much info.

Peta pulled herself up short. Someone was a murderer here, which meant that she *didn't* know the islanders anymore. And incredibly, Lawson had insinuated himself into this closed society and become an active part of it. He probably knew them better than she did. Yes, the truth was, she didn't know as much as she thought she did.

The cave, for instance. She'd lived all but the last ten years on this wind-blown rock and didn't even know there was a cave there.

Had it been a bunker, part of a trap for enemy subs, assuming that they'd made it across the Atlantic? The evidence certainly pointed to it.

Aunt Linda had blasted her once when she was about thirteen, for playing near the cliffs. By then, Peta had already learned that her aunt had no love for her charge, merely a love for the money her sister sent each month.

Peta found her lips tightening. She'd discovered later on that Aunt Kathleen had spied Peta coming from the driveway that led to the lighthouse cottage that summer afternoon and assumed that she'd been playing at the edge. In reality, she'd been pushing her fear of heights that day, testing it, trying to break free of it. Maybe even testing God. Maybe seeing if He would just take her life then and there for being such a bad kid.

Now, years later, and teasing out the memory, she wondered how she could have felt so defiant and angry at the Lord.

The distant memories of hurt slowly expanded into one single, clear memory.

She heard Lawson hang up, then another buzzer sounded.

"Peta?"

She turned to Lawson. He was holding his back door open as Long was stepping into the kitchen.

"What's wrong?" Lawson asked.

She frowned at the police officer. "I'm thinking that I don't really know these people anymore. And that I couldn't believe that I wouldn't know about the cave, or bunker or whatever it was that Joey mentioned. But I think I *did* know."

"How?"

"Aunt Kathleen caught me near the cliff one day, and Aunt Linda said something about how going near the cliff wasn't such a big deal anymore, but Aunt Kathleen had argued back. It was one of the rare times I saw them disagree. But Aunt Kathleen said something like 'loose lips sink ships.' I remember Aunt Linda saying that there weren't any more ships to sink. That there never were any."

"But they aren't old enough to have lived as adults through the Second World War."

"Aunt Kathleen is. She's in her eighties. My mother was actually a change-of-life baby. Anyway, I remember that Aunt Kathleen was really mad, and told Aunt Linda it wasn't ships, but visitors she was talking about. Too many would ruin the island. I thought that they were talking about me, that if I got hurt, Family Services would come and investigate and that was the one thing Aunt Kathleen didn't want. After all, Aunt Kathleen didn't even want me in her house."

"Maybe that was it."

"I doubt that." She looked toward the police officer, who was listening and waiting patiently for her to finish. "More like these islanders didn't want a lot of outsiders coming in. Haven't you noticed how xenophobic they are?"

Lawson answered, "They guard their privacy, and the pristine condition of the island."

"I can't blame them," Long added. "Northwind's a beautiful island, amazingly unspoiled. Last year, the meadow by the lighthouse was filled with wildflowers. Lots of brilliant colors."

She watched both men agree with her, voices calm and soothing. Was that how Lawson had managed to finagle his way into life here on the island, while just the memory of her youth sent people shunning her?

She didn't want to think about that anymore. Turning back to the officer, she cocked her head. "Is there something wrong?"

Constable Long looked grim.

Dread washed over her. Biting her lip, she swallowed. "What's going on?"

Long took off his forge cap. "I have some news for you."

Her heart tripped. "What kind of news?"

"Good, actually. First up, the woman who owns the Lilac Cottage Bed-and-Breakfast called to explain the mixup on the receipt. She apologized for her mother, and faxed me some info. You were right. You had spent June 30 on the mainland."

Her voice caught in her throat. "Thank you," she whispered. *And thank You, Lord.*

"And we were able to finally track down the operator of the *Island Fairy*. He agrees with the B & B owner. She called him for you, and he brought you here on July 1. Ironically, it took Danny's murder to find him. He'd been visiting his mother, but has decided to ferry people back and forth. I don't know if you've noticed that the media is here."

"We've noticed." And, Peta thought, she'd noticed something else. The islanders, who hated having strangers here, were, all of a sudden, inundated with them. They must be champing at the bit. But why, she had no idea. It had to be good for the few businesses here.

"Do you have any questions for me?" Long asked.

She focused her attention back on the police officer. "No. Just thank you. I guess I'm off the hook as a suspect now?"

"It would seem to be."

Still noncommittal, she noticed. Did that mean he didn't have another suspect? She glanced over at Lawson. Should he tell the police what he knew? About Marcano? Surely the police would want to know this, as well.

And what about the wallet? Shouldn't the police know about that? About what kind of person Danny really was?

They know, a small voice told her. And they're keeping quiet about it for some reason. She looked back at him.

"Oh, one more question, please," she said.

"Yes?"

"Have you found who shot at us?"

"What makes you think it was at you two?"

She gritted her teeth. "The fact that one bullet shattered the police car's windows, and only by the grace of God were we not hit ourselves."

"There were a few wild shots, too. Why do you think you'd be a target?"

Irritation streamed over her. "I've been fighting the accusation of murder, and until you showed up here just now, I was pretty much *the* suspect. Someone here wants me to shut up and take the punishment, I'm sure of it."

"Who do you think killed Danny?"

"Gary Marcano."

Both Peta and Long turned to Lawson. Peta blinked. She hadn't expected him to say anything about Marcano, and jeopardize his own investigation. And yet, he had.

He'd also been on the phone just before Long arrived. Who had he been talking to? What had he learned?

And, she suddenly thought wildly, her mind racing, did that mean that his own investigation was now over?

TWELVE

Lawson couldn't believe what he'd just said. Had it just come out on the heels of the relief he felt on hearing that Peta's alibi was finally being accepted?

Yes, relief was what he felt, all right. In those few seconds, he'd felt a flood of thankfulness and the flash of images of what could now be between Peta and him.

Did he actually think there could be something between them? Like love?

What about his family? The wallet still lay tucked in his jacket pocket. He hadn't yet found the strength to do anything with it. He'd seen the picture. But to look at it again? His heart went cold just thinking about it.

He stared at Long calmly, despite the roil of emotions within him. "Gary Marcano works for an organized-crime family in Boston. He's originally from New Brunswick, so he returns occasionally. He met Danny on one of those trips."

With his head tilted as he listened, the policeman stood silently. Lawson spied Peta from the corner of his eye, biting her lip. But he wasn't going to mention her. The fact that she'd introduced the pair was irrelevant.

"I believe that Marcano hired Danny to do some illegal

work for him. In light of the token we found at Danny's house, could it be that Danny had a lot of dirty money in the bank? Why else would he have hidden the token away? And where else would he have earned money but in Boston, doing work for organized crime? What if Marcano murdered him over it?"

"All good questions." Long folded his arms. "And how do you know all this?"

Lawson pulled in a lungful of air. "My investigator discovered it."

"Your investigator?" Long's eyebrows shot up. "May I ask why you have an investigator?"

"My family disappeared after witnessing a mob hit and Jan, my investigator, has discovered that Marcano and Danny were involved somehow. She found that Danny had traveled to Boston on and off and was seen partying with the local mob. It's driving distance away."

"That doesn't make him a murderer."

"When I saw the receipt we found in the cubbyhole in his house, I knew that he had to have been going there without anyone here knowing. I'd been keeping an eye on him, and he'd sneaked out without me noticing."

Lawson paused, his brows knitting together. "And that receipt was for a popular restaurant in Boston. He signed the bottom of it. There were days he didn't come out of his house, which was normal for him, especially when the weather was bad. But I think that on the days he was gone, he had the lamps in his house on timers."

"We did find lights on timers in his house. Could there have been any other reason he could have been in Boston?" Long asked.

"Jan thinks he was studying Maritime war history, especially pertaining to the Navy, which may make sense consid-

ering what we've learned about the lighthouse and submarines."

Long frowned. "You're losing me. What about the lighthouse and submarines?"

"The lighthouse was turned off regularly during the war,
when it's the most dangerous," Peta answered. "We think it
may have been to lure submarines in."

"Maybe they were practicing blackouts and saving electric-
ity," the officer suggested.

"The lighthouse was shut off only when the tide was coming
in," she explained. "We think it had some military importance.
There was a military presence on the island at the time."

"Why would that little bit of history interest Danny?"

Lawson held his breath, unsure of where this line of conversation was taking them, and unsure if he could even handle
what was going to follow. Danny was somehow involved in
his family's disappearance. Could he deal with whatever they
discovered?

Long continued, "We're getting ahead of ourselves here. I
know who Marcano is, and I know why you're here, Lawson.
And I know about the stash of liquor in the lighthouse. Is it
possible that Danny was selling it to Benny Melanson, who
killed him, then considered the stuff his property? He's the
only one who doesn't buy liquor, but still manages to get
drunk every weekend and needs to dry out periodically. I'd
like to get him into rehab. I know a judge who's just waiting
for something like this to happen, so he can have Benny
treated properly."

"Danny must have got Benny to do some illegal work, like
destroying evidence, and then paid him in liquor," Peta
mused.

"Which I dumped at the edge of the woods near where the

road swerved close to the cliff, and told him it would go into the bay if I caught him near the lighthouse again," Lawson said, focusing on the conversation and not his roiling emotions. "I don't know where he's hiding it all now."

The room went silent. Then Peta said softly, "And if Benny killed Danny, which I doubt, he could know something about your family."

Long rubbed his forehead and looked at Lawson. "So do you think Benny murdered them?"

"No. Benny's not a violent person." Peta shook her head. "If only we could find Gary Marcano. He might be persuaded to tell you where your family is, especially now that Danny's dead and can be blamed for their disappearance."

Lawson looked down at her. "That's a good idea. I take back what I said about you being naive. You have an aptitude for thinking like a crook."

"Gee, thanks." Though her words were light, he knew instantly that he'd touched a nerve. She could think like a crook because only by the grace of God was she not one.

"So," she began again before he could apologize. "Find Gary and you may find your family. If only we knew where he was."

"He could be hiding out on Northwind."

"Which may mean," Long finished for Lawson, "he could have been our shooter."

Lawson and Peta stared at him, until the officer added with a sigh, "But where is he now?"

After Long left, Lawson drove Peta back to the cottage. It was already after noon. He checked the place thoroughly, inside and out, before he let Peta enter. In the kitchen he looked down at her, then opened his arms. She slipped close enough for him to draw her in. He looked into her eyes, deeper than anyone else had ever done before, she was sure. In the next moment, he lowered his mouth onto hers.

The kiss was simple, short, and so very sweet. When Lawson lifted his head, he tightened his arms around her and buried his face into the crook of her neck.

All she could do was pray. *Lord, have mercy on us. What are we supposed to do?*

Finally, too short a time later, he eased himself away from her.

She watched him move toward the door, and suddenly, she didn't want him to leave her alone. "Tell me, how did you manage to fit in so well here? The islanders like you, and they don't usually like strangers. They don't want new people around here any more than they want me here."

"They don't want their island spoiled. They think they'll lose control of what little they have here if people come. But I wasn't a threat to them," Lawson noted.

He must have seen the disbelief on her face and added, "A few years ago, I met Pastor Martin at a men's retreat in Maine, so I had that connection here. When I came and rented from Danny, of course they were suspicious of me. The municipal office even asked me what I planned to do with the land I've rented and if I knew Danny personally. I said I didn't. I knew of him, that was why I was there, but could honestly say I'd never met him before."

"So they just accepted you without further questions?"

"Not right away. I began to volunteer at the church, doing outreach with the kids and helping seniors. And I didn't ask a lot of questions." He pulled out a kitchen chair and sat down.

Peta sat opposite him. "Wouldn't that have frustrated you? It went against why you were here."

"It did. There were days when I just wanted to grab Danny and throttle him. But Pastor Martin knew why I was here and he helped a lot. We were able to find out things about Danny, like his sudden interest in war history. And in the meantime, I started doing a search of the island by myself."

"Of course. That metal detector." She'd seen it in his dining room. "Is that why you didn't disturb the land around this house? It belonged to Danny and you must have wondered if he'd buried your family there."

The words caused a pained look to flit across his face. "I thought of that. In fact, that was why I didn't want any landscaping done on the yard. I didn't want my family scraped up like dirt. Besides, that metal detector isn't just any old device. It's a high-resolution imager that detects disturbances in the soil as well as denser particles. But to everyone here, I'm just spending my free time beachcombing. To the untrained eye, it's just an expensive metal detector."

"The very fact you had so much free time should have bothered the locals, I would think. I mean, Danny didn't do any work here. He just hung around and always seemed lazy in everyone's eyes."

"I guess my volunteer work here helped me. That and the Lord."

True, she thought. It was amazing how God worked. "You must have proved that you weren't going to ruin this island."

He blew out a sigh. "But the people here just don't realize that Northwind is already ruined."

After he let himself into his house, Lawson found himself staring at the metal detector. With it, he'd searched for his family everywhere on the island, except the pond. And underneath the island. His heart clenched. The high cliffs that led to the cave that Joey had mentioned were slick and steep, the waters beneath them swift and dangerous. No one went near them, not even Danny, and Lawson had watched his moves closely for a year.

But then Danny had been to the States without his knowledge. So he could have also been down in that cave, as well. He could have been anywhere.

Lawson's mind whirred as he realized that he should have checked the tide after he left Peta. These last few days, he hadn't paid much attention to it. And now as the day wore on, he couldn't begin to guess where it would be. Or where his tide table was, for that matter.

He wasn't usually this disorganized, but with all that had been happening lately, he'd let the mess get away from him. He liked his life kept orderly, his work systematic and logically accessible. Peta's appearance and Culmore's death had changed all that.

Remembering what he and Peta had discovered in Culmore's house, he dug out his cell phone and dialed Jan's number. She answered after the second ring.

"Hey," he began. "Have you learned anything more about Danny Culmore's bank account?"

Lawson had spoken to her briefly on his way to the police station the night Peta had been attacked. Jan was very good at her job. If there were anything to find out, she'd have discovered it by now.

"I have, actually," Jan replied. "The fact that he had a token made it really simple. Not too many banks have them yet, and the description you gave me made it even easier. I have a list of the banks around the world that use that brand of technology, but I went on a hunch to see what countries don't have extradition treaties with either Canada or the United States. And where any Canadian with a brain in his head would like to spend his retirement. Or even just a nice holiday."

"Someplace warm?"

Jan sounded decidedly pleased with herself. "Exactly. I started with the list of what countries wouldn't send him home, then focused on those countries that would appeal to him. Danny Culmore grew up on an island, so it's likely he would feel the most comfortable on one. Then I cross-referenced it with which banks use tokens and sure enough, one country's banks have just introduced the new security of tokens. There must be a bit of crime in paradise, if they need the extra secure number to access bank accounts."

"In paradise? Where was he headed?"

"He was moving to Vanuatu."

"Vanuatu? As in the South Pacific? Are you sure?"

"It's an island paradise northeast of Australia, with no extradition treaty. And far away from New Brunswick."

Lawson smiled. "I knew I'd hired the right person."

"And I can do even better. After checking the flight schedules, my assistant called the main airlines that services Vanuatu, claiming to be Culmore. Culmore invited Peta to visit him, and I think he planned to leave shortly afterward. My assistant said he wanted to rebook. After a few hits, he got the right airline. They were able to provide a great deal of information, and based on where he was headed, I was even able to find out at what resort he planned to stay. He'd rented a small condo on one of the southern islands."

"You're brilliant."

She laughed. "Of course I am. I then worked backward from Vanuatu. He'd planned to leave from Bangor, Maine, this coming Sunday."

"That's the day Peta said she was leaving. I wonder if he'd asked Peta here for one last goodbye."

"Beats me. You knew him better than I did. I'm faxing you

all the info I got. Maybe that can help you find out who killed him. But I'm not finding much more that connects him to Marcano, I'm afraid."

"That's okay," he answered absently, ready to ring off. "Wait. One more thing. Do you know where Marcano was at the time of Culmore's murder?"

"Ahh, now that's a whole different kettle of fish, as you islanders may say."

She laughed again, sounding even more pleased with herself for some reason. Jan was from the Midwest and was still mildly amused by the different mind-set of those on the East Coast. "Sorry. I just wanted to say that. To tell you the truth—"

A beep sounded. "Just a sec," Jan interrupted herself. "I've got the police on the other line. Hang on. It could be important."

Several minutes ticked by until she returned.

"You still there, Lawson?" Jan asked.

"Yeah. Just trying to sort it all out."

"Here's something you don't need to sort out," she said hurriedly. "Marcano has just been arrested!"

His heart tripped over itself for a moment. "On what charge?"

"A couple of misdemeanors, it seems. The police raided a nightclub that had been suspected of serving minors and by sheer coincidence, Gary Marcano was partying there that night. He's in custody, but not for long."

"Why?"

"Some big mob lawyer is already at the station." Her tone turned anxious. "Lawson, you need to come down right now and ask him where your family is. If you don't come, Marcano will be out on bail and gone. Maybe for good!"

THIRTEEN

Leave Peta? The whole idea sounded foreign, as if the words belonged to another language.

His stomach tightened, his mind raced.

"Listen, Lawson, when he was arrested, Marcano had credit card receipts for gas dating back several weeks in his newly leased car," she continued swiftly. "But he hadn't spent much on gas for the last month. His car was serviced three weeks ago and the mechanic who did the oil change wrote the mileage on a decal on the windshield. Marcano had only put on a few hundred miles, which is confirmed by the gas receipts that he signed. He's been in the Greater Boston area for weeks so I doubt he was on Northwind at the time of the murder. That could work in his favor for bail, you know."

Lawson felt his heart plummet. Was it true that Marcano couldn't have been on hand to kill Danny Culmore?

This meant that whoever killed him was still out there.

Still *here* on Northwind.

And still upset that Peta was determined to clear her name.

Jan went on. "The police want to interview you again. It could be your only chance to confront Marcano. Lawson, the police can remind the courts of your family, but there's no substitute for you being here yourself, as your family's advocate.

It would make national headlines, not to mention push the public into demanding that Marcano remain in custody. You need to come back!"

He swallowed. "I'm not sure I can leave Peta."

"You don't think she's safe?"

"Not completely, no."

"Then bring her with you."

Lawson contemplated that suggestion. But Peta would never go. She had too much wrapped up in this island, too many emotions to work out. And, he was beginning to see, she wanted Danny's murderer brought to justice as much as he wanted his family's murderer to pay. "She won't come."

"Well, so be it. She'll be fine, and you won't be gone long." Jan's tone discarded any caution. She wanted Lawson back in Boston. She'd worked on his case for over a year and wanted to see Marcano pay for his crimes as much as Lawson did. "What would she do to put herself in danger? Go looking for whoever killed Danny Culmore? Would she do that?"

Yes, she might. Lawson felt a line of cold sweat trickle down his back. She already believed that whatever Danny was involved in would lead her to his murderer. They were getting close, and Peta wouldn't stop now. She'd already said as much.

Behind him, his fax machine beeped to life. Jan's faxes were arriving, even as she talked on.

He needed to make a decision immediately. Leave or stay and watch out for Peta.

"Lawson," Jan was practically shouting, "did you hear what I said? About Marcano getting bail? I'm telling you, there is a good chance he'll be released on bail unless you come down here and face him! You can bring your family back into the spotlight. Sure the police could mention it, but if we get you here, popular support will be in favor of keeping Marcano behind bars, and believe me, public opinion has more weight than we realize. You may think the judge and lawyers do that, but the public has a lot of influence, too."

He contemplated her words, as he glanced around. His gaze lit on his jacket. In it lay his father's wallet.

"And," she added when she heard only silence, "you can face Marcano, ask him yourself where your family is."

Lawson had wanted that for months now.

But to leave Peta here?

It would only be for a few days, a voice within whispered. She'd be safe. And yet, the idea of leaving her gripped his stomach, leaving him short of breath.

Lord, I need Your help.

Peta found herself lured back to the bedroom window. She'd made a cup of hot tea, munched on some biscuits and prowled around the cottage. Now she was in the bedroom upstairs, standing near the window, peering out at where the trees began and to where she'd slipped off the cliff. At this safe distance, everything looked serene, and oddly, her heart wasn't pounding in her chest as it usually did.

How was this possible? Because of all that had happened? Lawson's family was missing, killed, even. Danny was dead, and a sinkhole had appeared, something related to a previously unknown cave in the cliff. And the lighthouse, too. It had once warned boats away from the cliff.

Always back to the cliff. The pieces of the puzzle were fitting into place, and, she realized, she didn't like the picture they were forming.

Picture—like the one taken of Joey decades ago? Someone had hung off the cliff to snap that one.

Or stood on a ledge. Could Benny have taken the picture of his cousin?

Was Joey telling the truth about the cave? Had Danny learned of it and decided to use it?

Was it even safe to go in? After all, Doc Garvey had ordered the sinkhole to be filled in, and if that hole connected with the cave, who knew what kind of condition it was in? Or even who could be there, hiding inside?

And how odd that the hole should choose that particular moment to collapse.

The explosive rumbling she'd felt when she was being attacked at Danny's house had shaken the ground, vibrated upward through the house and startled her and her assailant, too, enough for her to free herself.

Had it loosened the earth above the cave? Or destabilized the back of it enough to make it collapse? But why at that time?

Dropping the lace sheer back into its place on the window, she pursed her lips. Whatever annoying speculation she might have made no difference if she stayed up here. She needed to get down into that cave to discover what was there.

Even the mere thought of the drop down there brought a cold sweat and a tingling along her scalp.

The sun dipped behind a few low-hanging clouds moving up the coast. Great. Another bank of fog was sweeping in. So much for the nice weather. Whatever she decided to do, she had better make it quick.

Do it.

Go down the cliff and find the cave. Something happened there. Why else would Danny have become interested in it?

And someone had murdered Danny. Maybe for that very reason. Her eyes strayed to the cliff again. It wouldn't be because of any military secrets. The war had taken place sixty-some years ago.

Peta toyed with the idea of calling Joey again. He knew more, but wouldn't or couldn't say anything. Maybe going there without Lawson would calm Joey down and let him open up a bit.

She returned downstairs and picked up the phone. Lawson, ever organized, had taped to the receiver some important phone numbers, including the clinic's number. Before second-guessing herself, she quickly dialed the number.

Doc Garvey answered, catching her off guard. "Um, I'm looking for Joey. Is he there?"

A cool silence lingered before he spoke. "No. He's not here. I don't know where he is." He didn't ask who was calling. He had caller ID, no doubt. "Why did you need him, Peta?"

Panic suddenly swelled in her and she stammered out, "N-nothing. I just wanted to check to see if he was okay. You know, after what happened last night."

"He's fine. It was just a sinkhole and it's filled in now. Did you tell the TV reporters anything? They don't need to know."

How would he know that a TV reporter had come by? He lived up on the north end of the island, on a nice, quiet acre that had no view of the small village. Had the reporters approached him, as well?

Again, dread weighed heavily on her, and she muttered a short sign-off before ending the phone call. Her hands still shaking, she hurriedly grabbed her jacket, a flashlight and the pair of sturdy walking shoes she'd worn to the island. Then, as an afterthought, her cell phone.

Now or never. *Be with me, Lord.*

Then she hurried out the side door.

The wind had picked up. By the time she reached the cliff's

edge, she knew that the tide was still rising, nearly reaching its peak. Peering uneasily over the edge, she swallowed. Did it have to be so far down? She glanced around, spying that small log she'd tossed away while trying to climb back up on the day she fell over.

Lord, give me strength, please.

With a shake of her head, she eased down onto her knees and put her back to the water. She had to be crazy, following up on a hunch given to her by a man some people here felt should be in a special-care home. And in doing so, was now facing her most dreaded fear.

"I hope I'm doing the right thing here, Lord," she said out loud. "But I hope even more that You're with me."

She shoved the flashlight into the waistband of her pants, right at the hip. Sliding over on her belly, and snatching that poor bayberry bush she'd grabbed before, she shoved herself down until her feet dangled. Heart pounding, air stuck in her lungs, she eased farther down, cringing as she went. There must be—

Her right foot hit something solid and flat. Then, her left foot found the same surface. Still clinging to the long grass at the top of cliff, she spread out her legs. With a deep breath, she peered down her side.

A ledge. About the size of her desk at work. And sloping down toward the cliff, as if it were needed for extra security.

Slowly Peta set her heels down and, still clinging to the cliff face, turned herself around.

She waited for her heartbeat to slow to a reasonable pace, for the air to work in her lungs again, and then peered hesitantly over the edge.

Through a blur, another ledge appeared, farther down than the four feet or so that she'd had to travel to reach this one. With a deep breath, she turned and knelt, stretched out a leg and scraped down the cliff again, hating this section even more. No weeds and grass to cling to, and even farther to go. And leaving her feeling like cheese on a grater.

She found a small outcropping to grip with her sweating hands, and then, once she decided she wasn't going to fall, she felt her right foot meet something solid.

But her left foot swung wildly, finding nothing but air around it. Where was the ledge?

She tucked her left foot closer to her right and found purchase. Releasing her grip, she turned. She felt the cold rock stick to her hot, sweating back as she leaned against the cliff. Cool summer or not, she was sweating buckets. With a quick swipe of her palms against her pants, she looked down. This ledge was smaller, but like the one above, slopped downward into the rock face.

Effectively hiding the opening to a cave from passing boats below, she noted.

The entrance was larger than she expected. A short person just needed to crouch slightly. Yanking out her flashlight, she blinked. The fog was already rolling in, and she could taste the dampness on her tongue, feel the tiny beads of water slipping into her eyes.

Swinging the light around the base of the entrance, she bent down and stepped inside.

The floor of the cave dipped, following the ledge's angle, but in a more broken pattern. There was an odd, dank smell inside, something rather unpleasant. Peta kept the flashlight trained on the cave floor until her eyes adjusted to the dimness.

She shivered, stepped down again slowly as the cave's interior blossomed into view. Overhead, a few support beams tipped haphazardly, and several large hooks still remained in the crossbeam. One even had a rope dangling over it. At the base of one was a small wooden crate. The stamped letters RCN were still visible. Royal Canadian Navy?

Peta swung the flashlight deeper into the cave. A broken wooden chair had tipped over and was now shoved into the crook where the wall met the floor.

And deeper in, more crates sat.

They looked familiar. Where had she seen them before?

The lighthouse. A crate like those was in the lighthouse, and it had the strong, eye-watering smell of cheap liquor. A similar smell lingered here.

Benny must have moved his stash down here. Did that have anything to do with Danny's death, though? She shone her flashlight around again. Things seemed to return to this cave, so whatever secrets it held must be deeper in.

Peta decided right then and there that she didn't like caves any more than she liked heights. She moved past the boxes and directed the flashlight farther in, casting the beam overhead as it lured her gaze into the descending dark.

And onto a sight that cut deep into her.

They were wrapped in plastic bags, some tied with ropes, some taped. One bag was much smaller than the rest, and at some time, the bag had been torn, revealing part of its contents.

With a gasp of recognition, Peta turned, scrambled out of the cave, just making it in time to retch over the ledge.

She lay there a few minutes, waiting for her stomach to calm, all the while taking the opportunity to pray. Fervently.

Lord, help. Help! What do I do now?

Her frantic prayer repeated, and feeling less nauseated, Peta rose. Where was her flashlight? She must have dropped it inside. Forget it. The police could retrieve it.

That decision made, she reached up to grab the first ledge. She pulled herself up, finding only the narrowest of footholds. Taking a few minutes to catch her rapid breath again, she stretched up, grabbed grass and weeds and pulled herself to the open field.

She lay there on the cool grass for a few minutes. *Lord, what do I do? Have mercy on me. On them.*

She needed to call Constable Long.

And Lawson. Hands still shaking as she sat up, she unzipped her jacket pocket and dug around for her phone.

Once free, it dropped to the soft grass. She retrieved it, but couldn't punch in the numbers, not even the two on the speed dial that would connect her to Lawson.

Forget the phone. Just run to the police station.

She shoved her cell into her pocket, and struggled to stand. It took several attempts—her knees were sore and weak, her vertigo was having a field day with her equilibrium.

Only then did she look around.

The fog had rolled in with a vengeance, filling the air with thick, white soup, as dense as any she'd seen before. Swirls of it raced past her head. She turned, and turned again. Where was the cliff? If she wasn't careful, she'd walk right off it.

Biting her lip, she turned again and dropped to her hands and knees. Once she located the cliff, she'd be able to move around 180 degrees and walk toward the trees. Once there, she'd find the village easily enough.

A noise and an odd flash of light caught her attention and she spun around to face it.

Someone, holding a fog lamp and letting its beam slice easily through the soup, emerged.

Then another person emerged, this one closer to her, startling her. And another. They all towered over her.

But it was the one with the syringe who really scared her.

FOURTEEN

Lawson was still holding the phone, still listening to Jan go on about the media.

"Wait! Jan, what did you say about gas stations?"

"Hmm?" Finally, sorting out her thoughts, Jan told him about the receipts found in Marcano's leased car, and how the evidence pointed to him not leaving the Boston area for some time. Lawson blinked, finding all Jan had said only now sinking into his brain.

Jan paused, then added, "I said that Marcano hadn't driven his car much in the last few weeks. The police have it and from what I've learned, he didn't put many miles on it, nor did he leave the Boston area."

"So he couldn't have been here when Culmore was killed?"

"I believe I just said that. He couldn't have murdered the guy. I wish I could tell you who was responsible, but I can't."

Marcano couldn't have murdered Danny because he wasn't on the island at the time.

Someone else murdered him.

"I can't come. I have to stay."

"What about everything we've worked for?"

"If Danny's killer is still here, Peta's in danger. My family is dead, and I have to let go of my revenge."

A serious, heavy pause lingered. Jan shared his faith, loved him for it, and, he knew by the weighty sigh that followed that she would trust his faith as much as she trusted her own.

"You're leaving me with a lot of work, you know. I'm going to have to call the Boston police and tell them that you're needed there more."

"Thanks," Lawson answered, knowing full well that Jan didn't like it when her advice wasn't taken. "I owe you big-time."

He hung up. Someone on this island had killed Danny Culmore. And that someone had shot at Peta, trying seriously to make sure that she wouldn't discover the truth.

His hand still on the phone from when he spoke to Jan, Lawson picked it up again. He quickly dialed the cottage's number.

No answer.

He tried Peta's cell phone but the automated voice told him that the cellular customer was out of the service area.

Where could she be? The whole island was well-serviced.

There was only one place she couldn't be reached. Surely, she hadn't gone there?

Deciding quickly, he grabbed his phone, his spare key to the cottage and, spying the dullness outside, he turned and grabbed his jacket.

His father's wallet slipped out and dropped with a thud to the floor. Pausing, Lawson reached down and slowly lifted it up. It flopped open, revealing the photo of him and his brother. His heart clenched, his stomach twisted as he set it down on the desk.

As soon as he turned onto Main Street, the village went white before him. He'd been on the island a year and in that time, heavy fog had settled in on many occasions. Sometimes it just dropped like a blanket, as it was doing now.

Lawson slowed, then inched along the street, hating that he couldn't see a thing.

The café finally appeared to his right and he pulled in to park parallel to it. Walking would probably be safer. Before long, he found himself in front of the clinic. The lights were on, their glow only faint in the thick fog.

Maybe Joey knew where the cave was.

Perhaps Joey could tell him more about the cave.

Lawson trotted up the few steps and grabbed the clinic's door handle. Locked. He peered inside, but there were no patients, no one at all inside.

He hurried around the corner, his right hand skimming the damp clapboards to keep his bearings. Around the next corner, he stopped. Joey's kitchen door was just ahead. Lawson reached up to knock on it.

The door flew open, inward, with a large form stepping menacingly into the space where Lawson's knuckles should have connected with the steel of the door.

A shotgun then rose up into Lawson's face.

"Whoa! Joey! It's me, Lawson. What are you doing? Put that gun down before you hurt someone."

The fog swirled into the kitchen. Though it was supposed to be a warm July day, the dampness as well as the sight before him chilled him to the bone. Slowly, Lawson lifted his arms, palms out.

"Joey, I'm not here to hurt you. What's going on? Why the shotgun?"

"It ain't safe."

"What's not safe?"

"Everything."

Lawson shook his head. "I know I don't feel safe with you pointing that gun at me. And you know I'm not here to hurt you, so put it down."

"Why you here then?"

"I'm looking for Peta. I called her place and no one answered. I was walking over to the cottage and thought I would stop to see if you knew where she was."

"Where's your Jeep?"

"It's too foggy to drive. I didn't want to risk hitting anyone."

Joey frowned, then lowered the gun. Confusion danced over his expression and finally, he stepped back to let Lawson into his kitchen.

Lawson hurried in and shut the door, becoming even more thankful when Joey set the shotgun down on the kitchen table. The overhead fluorescent lights glared in the dull day. "Aren't you supposed to be working today?"

"I got the afternoon off. I only help with patients and clean up, anyway. Doc Garvey says I don't have to be there all the time. He said he would be there today."

"Doc Garvey's in the clinic right now?" Lawson's gaze turned to the locked door from the kitchen to the back of the clinic. "I didn't see him when I was around the front."

Joey looked confused. Peta had said one had to speak calmly to him, ask direct, easy questions that would require only simple answers.

"Is Doc Garvey in the clinic now?"

"I don't know. It's my afternoon off."

"Have you seen Peta this afternoon? Did she call you?"

Joey shook his head. "I took a walk to the cove. Doc Garvey said I should exercise more. But I came back when it got foggy."

"So she hasn't talked to you?"

"No," Joey answered slowly. The old man then threw a cautious look at the door to the clinic.

"Doc Garvey works today." Joey frowned. Then shook his head.

"He's not answering the door."

"He always answers the door, even when he's with a patient."

"The front door is locked."

"Doc Garvey locks up when he leaves."

This line of talk wasn't going anywhere. "Joey, do you know where Peta might be?"

"I told her to leave the island. It ain't safe for her. I can handle the trouble here, but she can't."

"What trouble are you talking about?"

"I can afford to lose my job. Doc Garvey says I should retire soon. He said I would have a good pension, so I can handle the trouble."

"What is the trouble, Joey?"

"Peta ain't bad. She's got a good heart, like Pastor Martin says I have. I can handle the trouble, but she would end up in jail."

"You're strong, Joey, yes. But what is the trouble?"

"The pills. They'll blame me for it. I heard them talking. They'll say I gave Danny the pills because he was mean to me, and wanted to be mean to Peta."

Lawson's heart leaped. "The pills? The ones that ended up in Peta's prescription bottle?"

"They'll say I got the pills and gave them to Danny. But I'm not that dumb. If I wanted to get rid of pills, I'd flush them down the toilet."

"Who's *they,* Joey?"

"The ones who want to hurt Peta. They don't want her here."

"Do you know their names?"

Joey drilled a hard stare at Lawson, surprising him with the vehemence. For one brief moment, Lawson wondered if maybe Joey was capable of much more violence than Peta believed.

"I don't gossip," he stated flatly. "Pastor Martin says Jesus didn't gossip."

"But if they want to hurt Peta, we have to stop them. And we can't stop them unless you tell me who they are. That's not gossiping. Jesus would want you to help her. If they want you to take the blame for hurting Peta, you should stand up for yourself. You may end up in jail. You can save both of you."

"No! Doc Garvey said I wouldn't go to jail. He said he'd keep me out of it."

"So Doc Garvey knows someone is trying to blame Peta? Joey, does he know who got the pills?"

Joey looked down at his hands.

"Joey, do you believe that hurting Peta is okay?"

"No!"

"Then, you think that hurting Danny was okay?"

Joey squirmed, shifted his feet and refused to look up.

"You don't, do you? But you understand why they killed Danny, right?" Lawson was working a hunch right now, and yet trying desperately to understand Joey's muddled thinking. "Tell me why it was okay to stop Danny."

"'Cus he was ruining the island with his blood money. He was treating us badly, and bringing in bad things."

"Like what?"

"Like liquor for Benny. Like making him do bad things for liquor."

Benny? Lawson had brushed off the suspicions that Danny was the local rumrunner. He looked at Joey. "What other bad things?"

"People who don't belong on Northwind. We've been here, through all the bad stuff, and this is our island. When the fish stocks dropped and we had to stop fishing, no one came to help us. So we gotta do it ourselves. We gotta keep this island good."

His eyebrows twitched. "That's good, Joey. Really good. But if they want to hurt Peta, that's not good. Right, Joey?"

"No. But I told her to leave and she didn't. Now they want to hurt her. Miss McPherson said they had to do something."

Lawson's head shot up. Kathleen McPherson? "When did she say that?"

"When I was leaving at lunch. When she came in to talk to Doc Garvey, and I heard her say they had to do something."

Panic swelled in him, choking his breath. "Joey! Do you know where Peta is?"

Joey looked up blankly, and even though Lawson had asked him that question before, Lawson could see a dawning of alarm only now rise on his face. "Is she at the cottage? Did you call her?"

"Yes!" Lawson forced himself to calm down. "I called her. But she's not there." He pulled out his cell phone again, and dialed her number, first the cottage, then the cell. The same as before. She wasn't answering either.

Joey stepped closer. "You gotta find her! They want to hurt her!"

"Who, Joey? Doc Garvey, Miss McPherson? Who else?"

The older man suddenly began to pace. "I'm not supposed to say anything. Doc Garvey said he'd keep me out of jail if I said nothing. I promised him. They have to keep this island clean and keep bad people off!"

"Peta isn't bad, Joey. They've made a mistake, but we can fix it. Did they say where they were going?"

"No, I'm not supposed to say anything!" Joey's voice rose, and soon, just jabbering and mutterings that made no sense followed. Ignoring him for the moment, Lawson turned to the kitchen window and, staring at the thick fog, pulled out Constable Long's card. He stabbed out the numbers.

Joey grabbed him. "She's at the cave! I'm sorry! I gossiped too much. Loose lips sink ships. We're supposed to keep quiet about the cave, but I told you, and Peta has gone there. I saw her. She's gone to see the bad things that Danny did and made Benny do!"

He plowed past Lawson, and threw open the door.

"Wait! Joey, what bad things?"

Joey turned. "Benny needs my help. He's sick, Doc Garvey said, and needs me to look after him. His sickness makes him do the bad things. I don't want him to get into trouble!"

Then he disappeared into the fog.

Lawson snapped shut his phone and hurried out, more confused than ever. Had Peta gone to the cave? Fear and dread swamped through him, as cold as the fog swirled around him.

He turned, got his bearings and rushed into the soup. A few minutes later, he had to stop, keeping his feet firmly in the direction he'd been headed. He called out Joey's name.

It was as if the fog had swallowed up all the noise. And yet, in the distance, he could hear a foghorn sound. It came from ahead of him. The water between Northwind and Grand Manan Island was dead ahead. He pushed farther into the fog, almost bumping into the trees that lined the cottage driveway. Moving to his left, he found the culvert and crossed it, hurrying with surprising ease along the short, narrow lane.

After bumping into several more trees, he finally broke free of the woods, just as the sun sliced through the fog.

It was lifting! As swiftly as it had descended on Northwind, the fog was moving on. It did that sometimes. Sometimes, the whole bank of fog stayed in one spot, defying any wind or rain, and if you were to walk ten feet, you'd be free of it.

Lawson walked along the edge of the cliff, and as he suspected, he'd stepped out of the soupy mix and into brilliant daylight. He hurried to the cliff and peered over. But saw nothing.

The fog was moving north, and he had no idea where this cave was. And what happened to Joey?

Lawson didn't have time to look for him. Rather, after a hasty prayer, he tore off toward the lighthouse, and once past it, raced down toward Danny's small boat.

Scrambling down the shorter cliff, he spotted the gas tank and lunged for it.

Once he hooked up the gas line, he primed the engine. Then he dragged the boat into the water, and jumped in. Starting the cold engine took several pulls, but after a few backfires and an obvious bit of flooding on his part, the motor kicked to life.

Lawson twisted the accelerator and the boat shot off. Once he rounded the southeast corner, he saw the fog bank receding farther, thankfully. It was harder from this angle to see any cave, he was sure, but if the cave had been used as a bunker, then soldiers inside would have had to see their quarry. He slowed the engine and began to coast past the area where he figured the cave would be. The raucous cries of a seagull tried to distract him. The bird swooped down, hoping for a handout of food. He ignored it as he shouted Peta's name.

A rope. Not the bright yellow nylon line, but a dull brown, hemp cord caught his eye. It was tangled around a small bush that was somehow defying the odds by growing on the side of a cliff.

There it was! A darker spot, a shadow that could only mean a deeper crevice. It was directly above the rope, and directly below some scuffed and torn weeds.

Caught on the tidal currents, the boat floated past. Lawson

killed the engine and, using the oar lying in front of him, he paddled the boat back about ten feet.

Satisfied that it was enough, he dropped the oar and threw out the anchor. When it caught, the boat swung around and banged against the rocks. Before Lawson jumped out, he ripped open the seat in front of him and pawed through the compartment until he found the flashlight.

His foot slipped off the slick rocks and into the cold water, but he managed to climb up to where he'd seen the crevice.

It was a cave, all right. Lawson clicked on the flashlight and arced the beam into the cave.

Peta lay in a heap just inside the entrance, her flashlight beside her.

She didn't look merely unconscious. She looked far worse.

He yanked out his cell phone, but his shaking hand couldn't hold it. The phone bounced once, then toppled over the edge.

FIFTEEN

Ignoring the phone, Lawson rushed forward. "Peta!" He bent down to check her breathing and found nothing.

"Lord, please, do something!"

He checked her pulse and found it weak but steady. Pulling her up onto his lap, he tipped back her head and blew into her lungs. Once, two, three, four, five—

She sucked in a deep breath and began a fit of coughing. Lawson threw back his head and banged it on the rock wall.

Her coughing subsided, she struggled to turn onto her side. Instead of helping her up, he pulled her into a warm, strong embrace.

She clung to him in return.

"What happened, Peta? How did you manage to get down here? Did you fall?"

She sat up, blinking. "No. I…" She stared at him, her eyes widening. "I want to get out of this cave, now! Get me out of this cave, right now!"

He nodded and backed out of the way, to stand on the ledge. Peta followed, clinging to the rocks in order to stand beside the cave. "I hate heights! I hate being in this cave! How did you get here?"

"Culmore's boat. Right there—"

The boat was gone. He leaned forward and peered to his left. The boat was slipping into the receding fog, down toward the wharf. "So much for that anchor."

"It's the tide. It's strong. Never mind that. Lawson, there's—" She pulled in her breath, as if wanting to say more, but was unable to. "I've been up this cliff once this afternoon. I can do it again."

Before he could answer, she was pulling herself up onto the next ledge. What about her fear of heights? With a shake of his head, he helped her up onto the upper ledge. Even before he had lifted himself up, she'd hauled herself up the remaining cliff with remarkable speed.

"Whoa! Wait, Peta! You weren't breathing down there!" He stooped beside her. "Did you hurt yourself? What's wrong, Peta? Talk to me."

"I'm dizzy. I didn't hurt myself. It was from the injection. Lawson, you—"

"What injection?"

She stared at him for a moment, then looked away, wetting her lips. She looked pale. Blinking, she lay back down on the grass, on her side, with knees drawn up. "The same stuff he gave me before. I'm so dizzy and tired. I shouldn't have climbed up here so fast."

"What are you talking about? Do you have another migraine? Did Doc Garvey give you another shot?"

"No, and yes."

The words were clear and precise. And deep. Lawson looked up. Walking slowly toward them was the doctor. He was carrying a black leather bag. And beside him was Kathleen McPherson, a rifle in her all-too-steady hands. Beside her stood Jane Wood, looking even more masculine in her overalls and plaid shirt.

Lawson stood, carefully. The three islanders didn't move.

"I warned you there was going to be trouble," Kathleen growled out. "Peta's not like her mother. She's not the type to give up and leave."

"Everything was okay until this guy got involved. It would have worked out just fine if Lawson hadn't taken an interest. The pastor said we could trust him, but I knew better," snapped Jane. "And you two thought he was harmless."

"He is," answered Doc Garvey. "He's only here to get over his family's death."

"For a whole year?" Jane snapped back. "That's ridiculous. There's more, I tell ya. More. I bet Danny stole from him and he came here looking for revenge."

"It doesn't matter now, anyway," Doc Garvey answered smoothly. "We'll get rid of both of them. The plan can still work."

"Of course!" Kathleen said. "We can say they got involved and once he guessed that Peta had killed her ex-boyfriend, Danny, she had to kill him, too."

"And turn this island into some kind of black widow hideaway?" Doc Garvey snapped. "That's not what we decided."

"He's right. That'll call even more attention to us," said Jane. "We'll take them both to the mainland and have them die in a car accident, away from here. No one will come here looking for answers."

Lawson stood gaping at the crowd around him. They were debating this as if he and Peta were a fixable little problem. At his feet, Peta rolled over and struggled to sit up. Her voice was slurred. "You fools! You think problems will just go away because you don't want them on the island?"

Lawson helped her up before speaking. "Actually, they would have, if you three had just left things alone."

"What are you talking about?" Doc Garvey snapped.

"I'm talking about Danny Culmore. He was planning to leave for the South Pacific. Maybe even fake his own death beforehand. If you'd left things alone, the whole matter of him and Peta being on the island would have wrapped itself up in a matter of days. And anything he'd done here would have remained unsolved."

His own words didn't hurt as much as he expected. *Thank you, Lord, for taking away my vengeance.*

He leveled a wry stare at the three of them. "By then, Culmore would have arrived in a country with no extradition treaty with Canada or the United States and the matter would have turned into a cold-case file and been forgotten."

"And I would have been long gone, again." Though her words were definitely slurred, her determined tone was unmistakable. She leveled her saddened expression at her elderly aunt. "I know you never liked me, but I'm your sister's daughter. Doesn't that count for anything?"

Kathleen lowered the rifle slightly. "She was trouble. And she always got herself out of it by blaming either me or Linda. She didn't care about her sisters, so why should I care about you?" She lifted the weapon up.

"I don't expect you to care for me, Aunt Kathleen. I didn't just come here to visit Danny, but also to apologize for all I've done. I'm not the same person I was before. And I kind of hoped you wouldn't be, either."

Kathleen's arms began to shake. Jane snarled out, "I'm tired of this. Let's do what we came here to do."

Doc Garvey opened his bag and drew out a plastic syringe. "This is getting expensive, you know. I only have so much of this drug and I've already had to split the dose."

"Just give it to him," spat out Jane. "Kathleen, hold that thing steady. You better not be having second thoughts."

Lawson eased Peta back to the ground. She stared up, her expression slack with confusion. He stepped away from her, moving away from the cliff.

"No!" Jane snatched the rifle from Kathleen and aimed it directly at Peta. "Get back here!" she shouted at him. "Down on your knees or I shoot Peta."

Lawson froze. He thoroughly believed that she'd carry out her threat. He wouldn't risk Peta's life. Slowly, he eased himself down onto the grass.

Lord Father. I need You now. We both love You, and we both need You now.

The Twenty-Third Psalm glided into his mind, and he began to quote it silently. *The Lord is my shepherd. I shall not want...*
...and I will dwell in the house of the Lord forever.

His life was nothing if he couldn't save Peta's. He hadn't been able to find his family, or save them. All these months, he'd wondered if going with them that evening might have perhaps changed the outcome. But it was too late for speculation. His family was dead. He knew it.

But he wasn't going to let Peta die. He glanced wildly around.

There was only one thing left to do to keep that from happening.

Peta fought the painkiller. She'd always welcomed the grogginess, appreciating its lure to sleep when migraines got the better of her. But if she dropped off now, she'd never wake up again.

A sharp movement caught her attention and she turned to her right. Lawson had grabbed the small log she'd spied earlier. At about three feet in length and solid enough to do some serious damage, it was a decent weapon.

But not against a firearm. Jane Wood could be nasty, and had been known to hold a grudge over things for years.

As she'd been. Peta cringed. She'd been angry with herself for years, knowing that she'd been awful to the people here, and deserved their resentment. Lawson was right. She'd given God her future, her love—everything, except her past.

She shut her eyes. *Father in heaven, I need You. I'm so sorry I haven't forgiven myself as You have. I should have been made new, but I couldn't let go of all the awful things I did years ago.*

Somewhere behind the mob, a scream sounded. Kathleen, wizened and yet still sharp, twisted around. Lawson took the opportunity and swung the log toward Jane. She dropped like a stone, and the rifle skittered away. Kathleen rushed over to it.

Peta bolted to standing, shocked by her own strength. She plowed into Kathleen and sent both of them tumbling to the ground.

Scrambling over her aunt, Peta grabbed the rifle. She could hear Kathleen cry out and then groan, but forced herself not to stop. Once she was several feet from the old woman, she climbed unsteadily to her feet and woozily aimed the barrel at the crowd.

But pandemonium had broken out. From somewhere in the woods, a blur drove past her toward Jane, who took the brunt of the impact and fell to the ground. Lawson tackled Doc Garvey.

Blinking, Peta stared at the men on top of the sturdy Jane. Joey and Benny? She'd never seen old men move so fast. Then, when he'd seen Lawson pin the doctor down, Joey snatched the doctor's bag and syringe from him. Benny locked Jane's arms tightly behind her back.

Within a minute, the small mob was nothing but a group of moaning, aching people.

A police siren sliced through the sudden quiet and when the

growl of an engine made everyone turn, Peta saw the police car skid to a stop. Trudy was at the wheel, but Constable Long alit first from the passenger side. Joey must have called them.

Still beside her aunt as the woman moaned on the ground, Peta sank to her knees. The medication kicked in quickly to steal her clearheadedness. Lawson strode swiftly to her side. Handing the rifle to Long, he pulled her into his arms and held her there.

"You did good, Peta. Very good, considering the drug in your system."

"It wasn't me, Lawson. It was God. I know it. Lying there, listening to Kathleen, I knew that I had never given God my past, just as you said. I gave it all to Him just now. It doesn't matter what I was like years ago. I'm not going to let it pull me down anymore."

"Atta girl."

She shook her head and tried to focus. Then, knowing she may not have much clarity left, she looked deep into his eyes. "Lawson? I love you. I really do. But there's no good way to say this."

"Say what? That you love me? I think you said it just fine. I love you, too."

She shook her head, finding tears clouding her sight. "No. I'll just say it. There's a whole group of bodies down in that cave, Lawson. Adults and a child. It could be your family."

His smile faded. He said nothing.

Tears slipped from her eyes. "I'm so sorry. There are at least three people down there."

"Five."

Peta and Lawson looked up at Benny, who'd come to stand closer. His face was pinched and he looked decades older than he'd ever looked before.

"There's five of 'em," he said softly. "One's a kid."

"How do you know?" she asked.

"I helped Danny put them there, and," he added after a pause, "I was down there this week again."

Lawson blinked. "Why didn't you say anything? Or call the police?"

"They were dead and at peace before I helped Danny. It ain't right to drag 'em back up. I was going to move them farther in, but my explosives damaged the cave. I figured I should just leave them alone."

"Explosives?" Peta echoed. She stared at Benny, wondering again if he was more like his less intelligent cousin than she realized.

Long, too, looked from the people moaning on the ground to Benny, and then Peta. Kathleen coughed loudly.

Lawson rose and knelt beside the old woman, whose ashen face showed her terrible pain. "Those people down there are already dead. These people need medical help."

Peta nodded. "Yes. I think Aunt Kathleen is really hurt. I may have broken a bone when I plowed into her."

Long blew out a sigh as Trudy called for backup. Doc Garvey rubbed his jaw and sat up. "Let me have a look at her. Trudy, you had better call the Island Fairy. He acts as an ambulance when needed, and I think we're going to need him today." He shot Lawson and Long a sharp look. "I may be an old fool, hoping to preserve this island, and keep it safe from scum like Danny Culmore, but I'm still this island's doctor."

With that, he stood and walked over to Kathleen, speaking quietly to her to reassure her. She looked pale and clammy.

Peta drew in her breath before pursing her lips. Then, with a growing frown, her gaze slid up the doctor's solid frame, to light onto his face with shocked understanding. "You're more than just an old fool. You're the one who tried to kill me in

Danny's house. I recognize the scent you're wearing. Cologne, plus a disinfectant."

She glanced down at his left arm. His short sleeve shirt didn't quite cover the square bandage on his bicep. She gasped. "That's where I bit you!"

His expression didn't waver. Cool, professional, so totally noncommittal and even challenging.

Her eyes widened farther. "And you killed Danny. You're the only one who could have. Physically, you're as strong as Danny, and you're the only one who could give him the drug. The one that ended up in my prescription bottle. That's how you knew which drug I take for migraines, which isn't the usual prescription. You weren't even surprised that I had it. I thought it was because my mother had migraines, but it was because you'd already seen my prescription bottle. But why go back in? You had a legitimate reason for being in the house before. What were you cleaning up?"

"I went to find his blood money. The islanders need it. Except, with all the dust, I sneezed and wanted to clean it up, in case the police came back and suspected me of coming back in."

"So why did you kill Danny?"

He leaned forward, his words for her alone. "I did it for Northwind. For this island. That's why I took Kathleen's rifle and shot at you. You were figuring it all out."

"All right, then," Long interrupted, hauling the doctor to standing. "We'll see to Kathleen. You're under arrest." He turned to Lawson. "I hope you don't mind that we don't go down into that cave right away. I have a feeling that we're going to be busy with this for a while."

Lawson pulled Peta into his arms. "I'm okay with it. Do it when you get a chance. But I want to go down there with you."

Peta felt the tears spring anew in her eyes. Sadness welled in her as she watched Kathleen McPherson be carefully shipped off to Saint John with a possible broken hip.

Peta noted with a small smile that the ferry operator recognized her, and reconfirmed that she'd come to the island on July 1, and not the day before.

It was after seven that evening when Long finally approached Lawson up on the cliff. He'd spent much of the time at Peta's side, offering a shoulder for her to doze on, right there in the open field's soft grass, after Kathleen was gone.

Peta straightened as Lawson rose. Long looked him square in the eye. "We're ready to go down into the cave. A forensic anthropologist has just arrived. She wants to be the first in to examine the bodies. That's her job with the police. Any bodies that have been left over a few weeks are best handled by her."

Lawson nodded, then turned to Peta. "You don't need to come."

She shook her head. "I'll come to the edge of the cliff. You'll need me to show you the best way down."

They all went to the edge. The fog had disappeared completely, and she spied Danny's boat, caught up on some rocks, the tide having turned now, pulling it back toward the Gulf of Maine.

The anthropologist, a middle-aged woman with a professional demeanor, followed Lawson down to the first ledge.

Peta eased closer to the cliff and met his gaze. His eyes were sad, and she wanted to jump down, fears forgotten, and hold him close.

But then, following the anthropologist this time, he disappeared onto the next ledge, and into the cave.

SIXTEEN

Lawson's heart was pounding hard in his throat, but at the cave entrance, he managed to hold the anthropologist's flashlight steady for her. She took a series of photographs, temporarily blinding him with the flashes. Then she stooped, and gently cut away the black plastic of the nearest form.

He blinked, and swallowed. The flashlight wobbled until Long took it from him.

Even before the plastic was completely gone, he recognized the crop of white hair as his father's.

He turned, and found Peta there, her arms open. She'd somehow climbed down without anyone noticing, and gone was the fear she's shown before. He stepped into her embrace.

A little while later, he looked over her shoulder into the cave and immediately recognized his mother's favorite scarf. He didn't look anymore.

They returned to the top of the cliff before the police boat anchored and handed up the rescue stretchers. Long climbed up after them, leaving the recovery to other officers better trained than he was.

"I'm sorry. The anthropologist says they've probably been there for about eighteen to twenty months. Last winter's cold weather and the cool summer so far have slowed decomposition. The ages and sexes of them match your descriptions. I need to take both your statements. I've already been talking to the Boston police."

"I knew it was going to be my family. I've been here trying to find them for a year. An investigator I hired suspected that Culmore had hidden them on Northwind."

"I'm going to need everything from you and your investigator. Why didn't you come to me when you first got here?"

"Would you have let me conduct my own investigation? It's not like the islanders here enjoy having strangers around. You could have been the same way."

Long shook his head. "That's the whole crux of this problem, isn't it? These people don't want anything to spoil their island. They got fed up with Danny Culmore's blood money coming here and decided to do something about it."

"Where did Danny get his money?"

"We believe he stole it from the crime family Marcano worked for, but we'll need to get some forensic accountants to sort it all out. We just know that Danny decided it was time for him to leave, so it may have been that people were getting suspicious."

"Did he kill my family?"

Lawson shook his head. "Based on what the Boston police say, Gary Marcano did. He's still in custody, by the way. But Culmore was the one who hid the bodies for him. He may have learned about this cave years ago, or at least the rumor of it, and did some investigating, then decided that it was a good place to hide bodies. He used his boat, and the old hoist that you saw in the cave from when it was a bunker."

"What about Benny?" Peta asked. "He knew about it. Are you going to charge him?"

"Yes. But we need to dry him out first and then he'll probably go into a substance-abuse program in prison."

"He said something about using explosives to move them farther into the cave."

"We actually got a decent statement out of him for once. He used to do excavation work on the highways, and had—would you believe?—squirreled away some leftover dynamite."

"He hasn't worked for twenty years," Peta said, her tone shocked.

"And the dynamite was that old, too," Long answered her. "When Lawson told him he couldn't use the lighthouse to keep his stash in anymore, he decided to use the bunker. That set everything in motion. He figured he'd move the bodies deeper into the cave."

Peta touched her mouth in shock. "Why didn't he just keep his liquor in his home?"

"He lives in a small house owned by Doc Garvey, and the doctor didn't want him to drink or even have liquor in the house, so he always just hid it. The crazy part of all of this was the dynamite. He kept it on his back porch and when he went down into the cave and found the bodies again, he decided that they should go farther in. But in order to make the cave bigger, he needed to blast it."

"He could have killed himself!"

"You'd better believe it. I think his mind's gone, unfortunately. And his dynamite was weeping, so instead of calling us to have it disposed of properly, as he knew he should have, he decided to use it all up. So the blast was even bigger, thus causing the sinkhole. Doc Garvey knew the sinkhole had to be related to the cave and that Danny was somehow connected to it all. That's why he ordered the hole filled in immediately."

Peta gasped. "That was also how I was able to break free from Doc Garvey at Danny's house. The explosion caught us both off guard."

"Yes, and the doc has admitted to killing Danny, as well."

"But why attack Peta, if she was going to be charged with murder?" Lawson asked.

"He panicked when he went back to tidy up. I'm betting that the plan was to kill Danny in the old gazebo and have the whole thing fall into the bay, hopefully destroying any evidence of murder. But Peta's appearance, and her discovery of the body ruined everything," Long told him. "So they revised their plans and sent the ferry operator on a wild-goose chase on the mainland, telling him his mother, who lives up north, was ill."

"After you reported the accident, the doctor had to think fast, so he put the drugs into your prescription bottle." Lawson filled in the rest.

Long nodded. "So when you startled the doc at Danny's house later, he made another quick decision and tried to make it look like you went back to destroy evidence, but had an accident. By now, he must have been panicking. And that was why he shot at you."

"When did Doc Garvey have time to change the pills?" Peta asked.

"When I took him into the house to see if there were any bodies in there," Long said. "We were separated for a few minutes, and your pill bottle was on the floor. The doctor was already wearing latex gloves, so he was safe from fingerprints."

A soft song tripped through the breeze, and Long pulled out his cell phone. He spoke for several minutes then hung up.

"That was about your aunt, Miss Donald. She's arrived in Saint John, and they say she's broken her hip."

Peta cringed. "I did that when I tackled her."

Lawson grabbed her hand and squeezed it. "She's an old woman and any fall would have caused the break. You had to stop her, just as we had to stop Jane and Doc Garvey."

"She's asking to speak with you," Long said.

"To blast me for hurting her, I'll bet." Peta pulled back her shoulders.

"She asked if you could go into the office at her house and bring a brown portfolio from the bottom drawer of the desk."

Peta frowned, pursing her lips. "I'll go with you," Lawson offered.

"We're all needed over on the mainland, anyway. You need to give your statement to the major crimes unit and I have to escort the rest of our little mob to the Saint John police. The car ferry is coming over right now."

"I'll take my Jeep."

Peta hesitated. "I know I need to face up to everything and deal with it, and apologizing to Trudy was a lot easier than I thought it would be. But going to see Aunt Kathleen will be hard." She straightened. "Still, she's my aunt, and I owe her an apology, even if she threatened to shoot me."

"You can do it, Peta," Lawson said. "You climbed down to that ledge to be with me, didn't you?"

She beamed at him, and Lawson knew that she had newfound strength.

"And remember this," he added. "You were a convenience to all of them, that's all. But they can never hurt you again. You're free of them."

"Free in Jesus. And I'm free of my past, and that was a bigger hurdle." She brightened. "Which makes me free for so much more."

He pulled her close. "Like loving me? Because I love

you. We've both let go of a lot, and made room for way more as a result."

Her eyes glistening, she nodded and opened her arms to him.

Peta met up with Lawson at the ferry back to Northwind. He held her close for a moment, telling her again how much he loved her. How wonderful to hear those words, and yet they were as strange and beguiling as her sudden desire to return to the island.

They took seats at the back of the *Island Fairy*. "How was your visit with your aunt?" Lawson asked.

"Odd, to say the least. Difficult for both of us, and yet, satisfying. We set aside our prejudices." She looked at him. "And she gave me the B & B."

Lawson lifted his brows. "Really? To just look after it while she's convalescing? Or permanently?"

"She's not coming back. If the judge agrees with the police, she'll get a suspended sentence and be moved into a long-term-care facility in Saint John. She wants to turn ownership over to me."

"I'm gathering she has no other family?"

Peta laughed. "You mean, to choose from? No, she doesn't. But I think she's regretting what she's done here. She was the mastermind of the plan to kill Danny, but not to frame me, ironically. Jane wanted that. Aunt Kathleen couldn't stand that he was benefiting from so much evil. He'd been flaunting it around the island. Still no reason to kill him, though. I think being so close to dying herself, Aunt Kathleen understands that now."

She tucked herself in closer to Lawson, and he responded by wrapping an arm around her. The wind didn't seem as cold today. "I think my short conversation with her at the café affected her more than we realized," Peta mused.

"You can almost empathize with her. But Doc Garvey is a different story," Lawson said.

"You saw him?"

"At the police station. He told me that he expects to lose his license, but would do it all again if he had to. There's no regret in him. He's a good doctor, that's the sad part of it."

"I saw that when we were on the cliff after the fight," Peta said. "He was willing to treat everyone who was hurt, and he was professional with me when I had my migraine. It's such a shame, really."

"He was a doctor to a small community and wanted to keep it that way. He believed you wouldn't be killed, just arrested for murder, so that justified framing you."

"All this to keep an island pristine and free of crime and mainlanders." She pointed to a TV crew van that was driving down the wharf lane. "It's certainly backfired."

"They were willing to tolerate a bit of excitement if you'd taken the fall. They expected the fuss to die down quickly. But now, it's worse than ever. The police and some archaeologists and even the military are going to be combing that cave for quite a while. They want access to the lighthouse, too, and all the information we found there." He toyed with her hair as the wind blew it around. "Enough about them. Let's talk about us."

Peta's heart tripped up. "Us?"

"Yes. What are you going to do with the B & B?"

"I don't know. I could sell it, but I've never owned any property before. It's kind of exciting, even if it's just a little inn on a small island." She eyed him. "What about you?"

Sadness clouded his gaze and he looked off into the distance. "I'll take my family back to Boston. I have some aunts and uncles who will want to arrange a nice funeral for them. Last year, before coming here, I sold the restaurant that my family owned. It was hard, because I had to declare them all legally dead. I used some of the money to move here."

He shot her a cautious look, one that made her heart squeeze. "I could stay here," he said hesitantly. "There are good people on Northwind, like Trudy, and Pastor Martin. But you have a job back in Toronto."

She smiled. "I may need some help from someone with experience in the hospitality industry if I'm going to run a bed-and-breakfast. And if there are going to be people coming here, they'll need a place to stay. Would you help me?"

"Only if you marry me."

She smiled. "A prerequisite? And they say *I'm* a difficult person."

"No, you're a person who's finally let go of her past. But you haven't accepted my proposal yet."

"Silly me." She leaned forward to peck a kiss on his lips. "I accept."

He settled back in the ferry seat, smiling into the ever-present wind. "Good. Let's go home, then."

* * * * *

Dear Reader,

Have you ever done something you regretted? Were you a not-so-perfect child? Did you take that regret and those childhood memories into adulthood?

In my story, Peta did. She couldn't let go of her past, going so far as to think she wasn't worthy of God's love, that her sin wasn't forgivable, despite "knowing" that it was.

Regret can hold us back. Guilt can hold us back. While it's not always possible for us to forget the mistakes we've committed, we can give over our regret and move on. God wipes our slates clean, and treats us like new beings because of what Jesus did for us.

You don't have to try to forget the past, but you should learn from it. Just as you forgive your children because you love them, God forgives His children and moves on. So if the Perfect One can move on, so should we.

And it's never too late. This world would be a better place if we learned to forgive as God does. And that includes forgiving ourselves.

With hope that you enjoyed my book,

Barbara Phinney

QUESTIONS FOR DISCUSSION

1. Peta believes she's unlovable and that God isn't able to provide any physical comfort. Is this true? How is it not true?

2. Peta wondered if God had sent her to Northwind to reach Danny for Him, or to save someone else. Who do you think God was after? Lawson? Peta? Anyone else?

3. Has anything in your life happened differently from the way you were sure it was going to be? Did it work out well for you, despite the fact you were concerned while it was happening?

4. Peta has a well-documented fear. How do you think a Christian should handle such an obvious, deep fear?

5. The islanders are very private and closemouthed. They guard their island almost with their lives. Is this a healthy attitude toward land and community?

6. When Peta was young and had decided to test her fear, she'd hoped to be able to break herself free of it, and had even challenged God to take her life. It hadn't worked out until the climax of the book. What was different?

7. Do you think that finally giving her past to God helped Peta conquer the fear?

8. What fear or difficulty could you overcome if you simply turned it over to the Lord?

9. Toward the end, Lawson must make a decision to either return to Boston to face Marcano, or stay in order to help Peta. Does he make a wise decision?

10. Is earthly justice important to you? Why or why not?

11. Lawson begins to reason that his family is probably dead. He gives up part of his hope that they are alive. Would you do that?

12. In the Bible, Jesus says, "Let the dead bury their own dead," meaning in part that the commitment to serve Jesus on this earth is short. Lawson reasons that he must let go of his family in order to save Peta, whom he loves. How do you feel about that?

13. Lawson doesn't know if Peta loves him in return. Could you do the same thing as he has done, even though you may be helping someone who might not love you in return?

> But now, this is what the LORD says… "Fear not, for I have redeemed you… Forget the former things; do not dwell on the past."
> —*Isaiah* 43:1, 18

* * * * *

And now, turn the page for a sneak preview of
WHAT SARAH SAW *by Margaret Daley,*
the first story in WITHOUT A TRACE, *the exciting new*
continuity from Love Inspired Suspense!
On sale in January 2009 from Steeple Hill Books.

PROLOGUE

A patrol car was parked on Main Street in front of Farley's Pawn Shop. Approaching her office across the street, Dr. Jocelyn Gold shivered in the cool January air, remembering the same scene only five days before—when Earl Farley had been found dead, an apparent suicide, in his office right below his apartment on the second floor.

Was the sheriff's department completing its investigation into Earl's death? Sheriff Bradford Reed hadn't been very supportive when Earl had died, but then the Farleys didn't belong to the elite of Loomis. After the deputy left, she'd called Leah, Earl's wife, to offer to come over if she needed someone to talk to.

Jocelyn pushed her office door open and entered, hoping everything was all right with Leah, who had instantly renewed their friendship from high school when Jocelyn had returned to town nine months ago. She quickly crossed to the window and opened the blinds to allow sunlight to pour into the room. After being gone for two days to speak at a conference in New Orleans on counseling children who were victims of crime, the musty smell of a closed office accosted her.

The blinking light on her phone drew her attention. When she played her messages, Leah's voice blared from the speaker. "Jocelyn, I need to see you. I've made a mess of everything. I'll catch you when you get back tomorrow."

Her neighbor's frantic tone heightened Jocelyn's concern. She placed a call to Leah's apartment. What was going on? A new development in Earl's death?

Please, Leah, pick up.

On the fifth ring, a gruff-sounding man answered with, "Hello."

The rough voice snatched any words from Jocelyn's mind for a few seconds.

"Who's this?" the man demanded.

She tightened her hand around the receiver. "Dr. Jocelyn Gold," she said with as much authority as she could muster.

"Sheriff Reed. Why are you calling, Dr. Gold?"

"Leah's a friend. What happened? Is she all right?"

"We don't know. She's disappeared."

Jocelyn jerked up straight. "Disappeared? When? I saw her on Friday night right before I left." Her friend had urged her to go and speak at the conference, saying that she had Shelby and Clint to support her while Jocelyn was gone a few days.

"She's been gone hardly a day."

"Foul play?"

"Don't know. Her brother seems to think so."

Jocelyn instantly thought of Leah's three-year-old daughter. "Where's Sarah?"

"Clint Herald has her."

Leah's brother had her daughter. Relief trembled through Jocelyn. "You might want to come listen to my recorder. She left me a message. She sounded frightened."

"You're at your office?"

Jocelyn sagged back against her oak desk, all energy draining from her. "Yes. I'll be here catching up on some paperwork."

"I'll stop by after I've finished up here."

Even after the sheriff hung up, Jocelyn held the phone to her ear for a few extra seconds. *Where's Leah? Is she okay? Does this have something to do with Earl taking his own life?*

In spite of Leah's urging, I shouldn't have gone. If I had been here, maybe she wouldn't be missing. I let her down.

She'd come back to Loomis to get away from crime. When she'd worked with the New Orleans police as a consultant dealing with traumatized children, the stress had made her long for a more laid-back place to live and a job in which she wasn't bombarded constantly with the horrors people could do to children.

Memories she refused to think about inundated her with the suddenness of a summer thunderstorm sweeping in from the Gulf of Mexico. She couldn't hold them at bay. Legs quivering, she slid down the front of the desk to the hardwood floor.

I let someone else down and he died. Please don't let it be happening again. A tear slipped from one eye and rolled down her cheek. She swiped it away, determined not to revisit her past. But the images of the lost child—and of her friend Leah—haunted her.

ONE

Several hours later, Jocelyn dropped her pen, her hand aching from writing up her clients' notes in their files. Glancing toward the window, she saw the patrol car still in front of the pawnshop. She stood, stretching her arms above herself and rolling her head to ease the tension in her neck.

A knock sounded, and sent her whirling around toward the door. She stared at it, not moving an inch. This time someone pounded against the wood, prodding her forward. She hurried from her office into the reception area and peered out the peephole. The sight of Sam Pierce stunned her. She hadn't seen him in months—not since she'd worked that child kidnapping in New Orleans with him. It hadn't ended well, and they hadn't parted on good terms.

Sam pivoted to leave. Jocelyn quickly unlatched the lock and pulled the door open.

Halting, the over-six-foot FBI agent glanced back at her. Dressed in a black suit with a red tie, dark hair cut short, he fixed her with his intense stare, his tanned features making a mockery of the cool January weather.

"Jocelyn, it's good to see you again."

The formality in his voice made her wonder if he was only trying to be polite.

"I'd like to have a word with you. Sheriff Reed said that Leah Farley left a message on your answering machine. I'd like to listen to it."

"The FBI is working Leah's disappearance?"

"Yes." He took a step forward, forcing her to move to the side to allow him into the office.

"Really. I got the impression from the sheriff he didn't think Leah had met with foul play. I'm surprised he requested your assistance."

"The mayor did. I don't believe the sheriff was too happy, but he's cooperating."

"Good, because I don't think Leah would run away and leave her daughter behind. She adored her."

"So you knew her well. Professionally or personally?" He wore a no-nonsense expression, as if they hadn't dated for four months right before she had moved to Loomis. As if he hadn't saved her life once.

Jocelyn waved Sam toward the chair in front of her desk in her office. She sat in her own chair behind it, biding her time while she gathered her composure. As a psychologist, she'd learned to suppress any emotions she might experience in order to deal with a client's problem. Sam's presence strained that skill.

"Personally. We're neighbors." She knew she was stating the obvious, but Sam's intense stare unnerved her, as though he remembered their time together but not fondly. He was one of the reasons she had come to Loomis nine months ago to open a private practice and teach a few classes at Loomis College.

Grinning, Sam threw a glance at the pawnshop across the street and said in a teasing tone, "Yes, I can see." Then, as though he realized he'd slipped too quickly into a casual friendliness toward her, he stiffened, the smile gone.

His sudden change pricked her curiosity. He didn't like this any more than she did. That realization made getting through the interview a little easier. She relaxed the tensed set of her shoulders.

When she had started seeing Sam in New Orleans, she had known it wasn't wise to date someone she had to work with from time to time in volatile, intense situations. Being a consultant on kidnapping cases in which children were involved had thrown them together over the course of the year he'd been in the Big Easy.

Jocelyn gripped the edge of her desk. "Look, I'm happy to let you hear the recording and I'll help in any way I can, but I insist on us putting our former relationship in the past where it belongs."

"Do you mean it? You'll help with this case? Because I was thinking we need someone with your experience." His frosty gaze melted a few degrees.

Although she now worked with all age groups, in missing-persons cases she'd only dealt with the children involved. "Well, yes. I'll help. But since children are my specialty, I'm not sure how…" She drew in a deep breath, realizing what he was asking. "Sarah. You want me to work with Leah's daughter?"

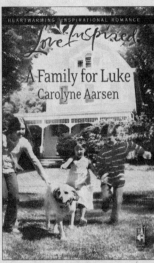

REQUEST YOUR FREE BOOKS!

2 FREE RIVETING INSPIRATIONAL NOVELS
PLUS 2 FREE MYSTERY GIFTS

YES! Please send me 2 FREE Love Inspired® Suspense novels and my 2 FREE mystery gifts (gifts are worth about $10). After receiving them, if I don't wish to receive any more books, I can return the shipping statement marked "cancel". If I don't cancel, I will receive 4 brand-new novels every month and be billed just $4.24 per book in the U.S. or $4.74 per book in Canada, plus 25¢ shipping and handling per book and applicable taxes, if any*. That's a savings of over 20% off the cover price! I understand that accepting the 2 free books and gifts places me under no obligation to buy anything. I can always return a shipment and cancel at any time. Even if I never buy another book, the two free books and gifts are mine to keep forever.

123 IDN ERXX   323 IDN ERXM

Name	(PLEASE PRINT)	
Address		Apt. #
City	State/Prov.	Zip/Postal Code

Signature (if under 18, a parent or guardian must sign)

Order online at www.LoveInspiredSuspense.com
Or mail to Steeple Hill Reader Service:

IN U.S.A.: P.O. Box 1867, Buffalo, NY 14240-1867
IN CANADA: P.O. Box 609, Fort Erie, Ontario L2A 5X3

Not valid to current subscribers of Love Inspired Suspense books.

Want to try two free books from another series?
Call 1-800-873-8635 or visit www.morefreebooks.com

* Terms and prices subject to change without notice. N.Y. residents add applicable sales tax. Canadian residents will be charged applicable provincial taxes and GST. Offer not valid in Quebec. This offer is limited to one order per household. All orders subject to approval. Credit or debit balances in a customer's account(s) may be offset by any other outstanding balance owed by or to the customer. Please allow 4 to 6 weeks for delivery. Offer available while quantities last.

Your Privacy: Steeple Hill Books is committed to protecting your privacy. Our Privacy Policy is available online at www.SteepleHill.com or upon request from the Reader Service. From time to time we make our lists of customers available to reputable third parties who may have a product or service of interest to you. If you would prefer we not share your name and address, please check here. ☐

LISUS08R

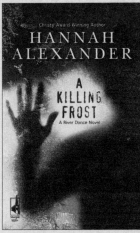

Love Inspired®
SUSPENSE

TITLES AVAILABLE NEXT MONTH

Don't miss these four stories in January

HEART OF THE NIGHT by Lenora Worth
When secret agent Eli Trudeau discovers his son is alive, he's furious with Gena Malone, the boy's adoptive mother. Yet even his anger can't blind him to Gena's love for the boy. And when someone dangerous comes after them, Eli will do *anything* to protect his newfound family.

WHAT SARAH SAW by Margaret Daley
Without a Trace

The three-year-old witness is FBI agent Sam Pierce's best resource when the girl's mother vanishes. Yet child psychologist Jocelyn Gold will barely let him near Sarah. Or herself. But for the child's sake—and her mother's—Sam and Jocelyn must join forces to uncover just what Sarah saw.

BAYOU BETRAYAL by Robin Caroll
Monique Harris has found her father—in prison for murder. Still, when Monique is suddenly widowed, she seeks refuge in the bayou town of Lagniappe, not knowing *someone* doesn't want her to stay. Deputy sheriff Gary Anderson has Monique hoping for a new future... if she can lay the past to rest.

FLASHOVER by Dana Mentink
Firefighter Ivy Beria is frustrated when she's injured on the job...until she realizes the fire was no accident. The danger builds when her neighbor disappears. With the help of friend and colleague Tim Carnelli, Ivy starts searching for answers, but she might find something more—like love.

LISCNM1208BPA